THE FORSAKEN MAID'S SECRET

Victorian Romance

FAYE GODWIN

Tica House Publishing

Sweet Romance that Delights and Enchants!

Copyright © 2019 by Faye Godwin

All rights reserved.

No part of this book may be reproduced in any form or by any electronic or mechanical means, including information storage and retrieval systems, without written permission from the author, except for the use of brief quotations in a book review.

PERSONAL WORD FROM THE AUTHOR

Dearest Readers,

I'm so delighted that you have chosen one of my books to read. I am proud to be a part of the team of writers at Tica House Publishing. Our goal is to inspire, entertain, and give you many hours of reading pleasure. Your kind words and loving readership are deeply appreciated.

I would like to personally invite you to sign up for updates and to become part of our **Exclusive Reader Club**—it's completely Free to Join! I'd love to welcome you!

Much love,

Faye Godwin

FAYE GODWIN

VISIT HERE to Join our Reader's Club and to Receive Tica House Updates:

https://victorian.subscribemenow.com/

PART I

CHAPTER 1

Bincy clung to her mother's hand as they moved through the street. Mama was walking quickly today; her scarf was pulled tightly around her throat, her hat low over her eyes, and Bincy had to hurry to keep up. Running made her chest burn a little, but she knew Mama had a reason for being in a hurry.

"Where are we going, Mama?" she asked, pausing to cough.

Mama looked down at her. Her mother's eyes had been blue once, but the pressure of hardship seemed to have squeezed the color out of them; now they were watery and gray, just like the weather.

"Just to buy something for dinner," she said, with a quick smile.

"Dinner?" Bincy's heart leapt. "Oh, that'll be nice, Mama. I'm so hungry."

"I know you are, darling." Mama sighed. She gave Bincy's arm a little tug. "You and all four of your siblings, just like you've been for the seven months since your papa..." She stopped.

"Why did he leave?" asked Bincy. "Where did he go?"

"I've told you and told you. Where he went, I don't know," said Mama shortly. "I don't want to know, either. And as for why he left, I suppose we were just one problem too many for him." Her voice was bitter.

Bincy held Mama's hand more tightly. "I'm sorry I made you sad."

"It's not your fault," said Mama with a long sigh.

"I'm not gonna think about him," said Bincy, trying to make her mother feel better. "Let's think about the nice dinner we're going to have soon. We're going to all sit and eat together, and it's going to be nice. We haven't had anything all day, but now we're all going to go to bed with full tummies."

To Bincy's surprise, a tear sneaked out of the corner of Mama's eye. She dashed it away quickly, but Bincy had seen it. "Why are you crying?" she asked, scared. The last time Mama had cried had been when Bincy's little brother, Jack, had died in the night. "Is someone dead?"

"No, no, my darling. Nothing like that," said Mama. "Hush now. Just hush and walk with me, there's a good girl."

Bincy obeyed, holding Mama's hand as they reached the outskirts of the slum where they lived. Everyone in the area had grown used to the smell; it was a strangely dynamic thing, changing every morning and every time the wind blew, alternately bringing whiffs in from the rotting Thames or the deep reek from the factories that bordered one side of the slum.

The streets themselves had their own special smell, too. There was no horse manure in the street; instead, the animal excrement that lay there was of a more noxious nature, mingled with the rotting carcasses of rats and mice. There was no rotten food lying in the streets, either. Someone would have picked it up and devoured it, regardless of how bad it was. Bincy knew this because there had been days when she would happily have been that someone.

But today wasn't going to be one of those days. They were going to buy dinner, Mama had said. They left the slum behind and headed toward the marketplace. Bincy managed a skip or two as she kept pace with her mother.

The marketplace was bustling. Bincy stuck close to Mama's skirt as they wove their way through the crush of bodies, staring around wide-eyed at the open square and the shops that lined it. There was a grocer, and a baker, and even a seamstress. Bincy liked the bright colors of the dresses proudly displayed in the window. She knew better than to ask

Mama if she could have one, though. Instead, she decided to set her hopes on the fragrant loaves of fresh bread that stood stacked in golden rows in front of the bakery.

"Are we going to get one of those, Mama?" she asked.

Mama seemed distracted. "Hmm? What?"

"One of those loaves, Mama. Are we going to get one of them for dinner?"

"Oh. Yes, dear. Whatever you like," Mama replied.

She had come to a halt in the middle of the square and was looking around, seeming lost. Bincy tugged her hand, moving toward the bakery. "Come on, Mama," she said. "I'm hungry."

Mama yanked Bincy back. "Come here," she said, a little cross. Closing her eyes, she took a deep breath, then knelt down. Her expression was gentler now as she looked into Bincy's eyes. She looked utterly exhausted; even the wisps of gray hair that dangled down on either side of her face looked drained and lifeless, like the frayed ends of a carpet that was reaching the end of its useful life.

"I'm sorry, Mama," Bincy whispered.

Mama shook her head, and Bincy thought she saw another tear fall as her mother straightened and quickly kissed the top of her head.

"No, dear," she said softly. "I'm sorry. Now, why don't you go to the bakery and pick out a loaf for dinner?"

"Yes!" Bincy bounced up and down with excitement. "I'm going to take the biggest one, Mama! The biggest one of them all!"

She pulled impatiently loose from Mama's hand and ran over to the bakery. The loaves were plump and round, their crusts baked to golden perfection, and Bincy's eyes immediately found the biggest one. She stood on tiptoe, pointing at it. "That one, Mama! Let's get that one. We'll all eat until we explode. Come on, let's buy it. Mama?"

Bincy turned around, and her entire world seemed to lurch with horror. Mama was nowhere to be seen. She spun around, looking everywhere, but the world was filled from one edge to the other with a crush of faceless strangers.

"Mama!" Bincy screamed. "MAMA! Where are you?" She ran into the crowd, the bread forgotten, pushing and shoving despite the angry voices around here. "Mama!" she shrieked. "MAMAAAA!"

Then, with a relief so great it almost brought her to her knees, Bincy spotted her. She was standing on the other end of the square, talking to a tall man in a police uniform. Bincy stumbled out of the crowd, breathless. She tried to scream for her mother, but a fit of coughing overwhelmed her, bending her double. She coughed and retched, her eyes streaming, but didn't look away from Mama.

Mama had heard her, but she wasn't coming closer. Instead, she just pointed at Bincy, saying something to the policeman.

He looked at Bincy and gave one curt nod. Then he walked toward her – and Mama turned her back and walked away.

Bincy caught her breath at last.

"Mama!" she screamed, rushing forward, the coughs coming again, grasping her, overwhelming her. "Mama," she gasped, but the word was a choked little thing, a wisp on the edge of her gasping breaths.

The policeman was almost upon her, but Bincy ignored him, staggering toward the place where her mother had disappeared into the crowd. He lunged at her, and she dodged, giving a scream of panic before running again, but her short limbs were no match for his. In one stride, he'd caught up with her, and a strong fist closed on her arm, yanking her back.

"No!" Bincy slapped at him, panicking. "Let me go! I need my mama!"

"Yeah, yeah, I know," growled the policeman, shaking off her hands effortlessly. "We're going to find your mama. That woman said she went this way."

"She's my mama," Bincy gasped, breathless with exertion. She grabbed the policeman's sleeve, staring up at him. "She's my mama."

"Yeah, I told you, we'll find her," said the policeman angrily. His eyes were darting, and he had a stubbly beard crawling over his double chin.

"No. *That* was my mama!" Bincy pointed in the direction Mama had gone.

The policeman's eyes widened. He straightened up, searching through the crowd, and spat a curse word. "She fooled me," he snapped. "Stupid woman! Now what am I supposed to do with you?"

"Find my mama!" Bincy clung to his sleeve, tears cascading down her cheeks. "Go find my mama! I need my mama!"

"Hush now!" snapped the policeman, giving her a firm shake that rattled her teeth. "Be quiet so that I can think."

"I want my mama!" Bincy wailed.

The policeman's slap came out of nowhere. It rang across her face, the shock – more than the pain – making Bincy freeze. No one had ever hurt her before. She stared up at the policeman, her tears instantly dried up with fright. His mouth was twisted with distaste.

"I should just let you go," he grumbled. "You can go looking for your good-for-nothing mother yourself. She probably dumped you because she doesn't know who your father is."

"Papa's gone," Bincy whispered. "I need Mama."

The policeman looked like he was about to slap her again. Bincy cowered, and then a bright voice spoke from somewhere behind her. "What's going on here, Thompson?"

Bincy saw the policeman flinch a little. He straightened. "Child abandoned in the marketplace, sir."

"Abandoned, you say?" Another policeman came into view. This one was older; he had a thatch of white hair, and something about his brown eyes made Bincy want to run to him. He looked like someone's grandfather.

"Yeah. Some woman came over and told me that there was a child wandering around the marketplace. She pointed the child out and pushed off. Turns out she was the mother."

"Oh, dear me." The older policeman's voice was gentle. He knelt in front of Bincy, studying her with pity. "What are we going to do with you, then, little one?"

Bincy had put her fist in her mouth. She sucked on it, staring at the policeman.

"Where did your mama go, love?" the policeman asked.

"That way," whispered Bincy, pointing.

The policemen exchanged glances. "She'll be long gone," said the younger one. "We'll never find her again."

"You *have* to find her," cried Bincy. "I need her."

"Hush, little one." The older policeman took her hand, gently pulling her away from the younger. "It's all right. You're going to come with me, and I'll take you somewhere safe, understand? You're going to be all right."

"What about my mama?" asked Bincy.

She could see heartache in the policeman's eyes. "Your mama isn't here to take care of you right now," he said gently. "So, we're going to take you to someone who can. Come on, love. It's going to be all right. You'll see – everything is going to be all right."

Bincy didn't know what else to do, so she took the policeman's hand, and she believed him.

CHAPTER 2

Bincy's little head lolled on the policeman's shoulder. She hadn't walked far before he'd picked her up and put her on his hip, but her legs still ached with exhaustion, and she could feel her breaths gurgling in her lungs. She felt hot, and she just wanted her mama. But she was too tired to fuss and cry. She gazed listlessly at the houses the policeman was passing as he walked along the street, bearing Bincy's weight easily on one strong arm.

"I wouldn't have picked her up if I were you," said the younger policeman, who walked beside them. "Think of the lice."

"Nothing that a good bath won't fix," said the older policeman. "Something you haven't had in a while, have you, little one? Well, here you're going to get cleaned up and fed, and you'll feel much better in a minute."

Bincy looked up. They had reached a tall, gray building surrounded by a high palisade fence; it was topped with spikes, and they made Bincy tremble a little as the policeman walked up to the gate. The younger policeman held it open, and Bincy was carried inside. The gate swung shut behind them, and the younger policeman pushed the bolt through with a clang that held a flat finality.

The oak door was protected by an iron grille, and the policemen had to knock and stand on the doorstep for a long minute before there were footsteps from deep inside the house. They echoed as if the walker was moving along a huge, empty hallway.

"Where are we?" Bincy whimpered.

"We're at a place that looks after little children like you," said the older policeman soothingly.

The door swung open. The hall was just as giant and lonely as Bincy had imagined, and in the doorway stood a woman so thin and severe that she looked more like a breadknife than a human being. Her hair was cropped close to her head, and her black dress clung miserably to her figure as if it had no other choice. Her nose was sharply hooked, but the eyes were dull and exhausted as they traveled from the policeman to Bincy and back again.

"Another one?" sighed the woman. "When will you stop bringing me foundlings, Bert?"

"Where else should I take them?" asked the older policeman softly. "I can't imagine a little mite like this stuck in a workhouse, Agatha. You know I can't do that."

"I suppose I do," said the woman.

"Do you have room?" asked Bert.

"I do, but only for one more," said the woman. "You'll have to put her down. I can't pick them up anymore, not with my back."

Bert gently lowered Bincy to the floor. Instantly, she clung to his arm with a shriek. "No! Don't let me go!" she cried. "I want my mama. Please, take me to my mama!"

"You have to go with this nice lady now," said Bert. "This is Mrs. Price, and she's going to take good care of you. You don't have to worry, little one."

"I want Mama!" screamed Bincy. "Where is Mama? Take me to Mama!"

"Your mama isn't here now," Bert began, but Mrs. Price interrupted him.

"Trust me, it's no use," she said impatiently, grabbing Bincy's arm. "There's nothing you can do to make it better. Just go back to work, Bert. And try not to come across any more lost children for a few months."

Bert stared at Bincy, agonized. "She's so frightened," he said, gently pulling his arm away.

"NO!" shrieked Bincy. "MAMA! COME BACK!"

"Go, Bert," said Mrs. Price, towing Bincy inside. "Just go." She slammed the door, and Bincy threw herself against it, desperate to be free from the strange new place.

"Come BACK!" she screamed. "Please!"

"Hush now!" snapped Mrs. Price.

Bincy cowered, expecting another blow. Instead, Mrs. Price pulled her to her feet and knelt down to face her, although it seemed to be an effort. Her eyes studied Bincy with a mixture of annoyance and sorrow.

"Listen to me, girl," she said. "Your mama's gone. She's not coming back. Now you have to be a good girl and come with me, then things won't be so bad."

"But..." Bincy began.

"Now, tell me your name," ordered Mrs. Price.

Her voice was so commanding that Bincy didn't feel she had another option. "Bincy," she whispered. "Bincy Hall."

"Good. And how old are you?"

"Seven," Bincy murmured.

Mrs. Price sighed. She suddenly looked so tired. "Come along, then." She rose stiffly, taking Bincy's small hand in her own. Her grip was cold and bony. "It's getting late. Are you hungry?"

Wide-eyed, Bincy nodded fervently.

"Of course, you are." Mrs. Price shook her head. "Let's get you something to eat. Does that sound good to you?"

"Yes," Bincy whispered. But as Mrs. Price led her down into the dark hallway, Bincy couldn't help looking back over her shoulder at the door.

She still wanted her mama.

THE SOUP WAS THE MOST MAGICAL THING BINCY HAD EVER tasted. There were vegetables in it and even a few chunks of meat, and Bincy found herself choking it down as fast as she could, distracted from her fear by the way it warmed her from the inside out. She went through two bowls of it before finally, breathless and so full she could barely move, she stopped.

Bincy's belly was full, but the eating hall around her yawned with emptiness. The walls were a bleak gray, the hall itself filled with rows of straight wooden tables with uncomfortable benches. Bincy had never been inside such a large building. She set the empty bowl down on the table and looked up nervously at Mrs. Price, who was standing nearby, watching her critically.

"Thank you," she said quietly.

"Good. Now, time for bed," said Mrs. Price.

This time, she didn't take Bincy's hand as she led her back out of the eating hall. Bincy wanted to grab her skirt as they walked down another hallway, but she didn't have the courage. Instead, she asked in a whisper, "What is this place?"

"It's an orphanage, Bincy," said Mrs. Price. Seeing Bincy's blank look, she sighed, relenting slightly. "A place for children who don't have mamas anymore to live with."

"But I do have a mama," said Bincy. "When can I see her? When is she coming to get me?"

Mrs. Price paused outside a closed door. She looked down at Bincy, and the little girl thought she might have seen a tear in Mrs. Price's harsh eye. For a long moment, Bincy waited for the old lady to say something. Instead, Mrs. Price just squared her shoulders and opened the door.

"This is your room," she said.

Bincy stepped inside. The room was almost as big as the entire tenement where she lived with her mother and four siblings, and nearly as crammed. There were two bunk beds pushed up against the furthest corners of the room, and the square of light that fell into the room through the opened door prompted three faces to peer out from beneath the covers on the beds.

"June, Fran, Mae, this is Bincy," said Mrs. Price. "She's going to stay in your dormitory room with you."

"Does she have to?" asked one of the girls, sounding irritated.

"Don't make me remind you of your place, Mae," snapped Mrs. Price, her eyes flashing. "Now, go to bed, Bincy. Stay quietly in your bunk until the bell rings tomorrow morning."

Bincy turned, grasping at Mrs. Price's skirt in panic, wanting to shout for her not to go. But the old woman had already disappeared, and the door shut behind her with a click. Trembling a little, Bincy made her way to the nearest bunk. The bottom bunk was empty, but there was a tousle of black hair on the pillow of the top one.

"Excuse me," Bincy said, tugging at the covers. Her hands were trembling.

The occupant of the bunk flipped over and fixed Bincy with a glare.

"What do you want?" the older girl demanded.

"Can I climb into bed with you?" Bincy whimpered. "I'm cold and scared."

The girl stared at her for a moment, and Bincy's heart thumped hard. She was so afraid of lying in a bed all by herself in this dark and unfamiliar night. Then the girl seemed to relent, shifting up a little.

"Sure," she said. "Get in."

"Thank you." Bincy scrambled part of the way up the ladder, reaching out for the mattress. Her hands had just touched its rough surface when a foot was planted squarely in her chest. With a yelp of fright, she fell backwards, landing heavily on the floor, bottom first. The pain and fear brought tears back to her eyes, and she felt them coursing down her cheeks as she stared mutely at the girl on the top bunk.

The girl laughed. "Did you really think I was going to let a lousy little thing like you into my bed?" she demanded. "Go away. We don't want you here."

Sniveling, Bincy realized she had no choice. She crawled into the bottom bunk; compared to her sleeping pallet back at home, the hard, straw mattress was soft. It brought her no comfort, though, as she rolled herself in her blanket and buried her face in the lumpy pillow. Sobs tore at her body. She missed her mama's warm curves so much, even missing the quarreling tangle of limbs that their bed often became when all of her siblings were in it as well.

"Hey, new girl!" barked another of the older girls.

Bincy looked up, her sobs frightened into silence.

"Try to cry quietly," the girl snapped. "We're trying to sleep here."

There was a ripple of cruel giggles from the other girls, and

Bincy wedged herself more deeply into her bed, trying to muffle the sobs that welled up from the deepest part of her soul.

CHAPTER 3

Bincy clung to Mae's skirt for dear life as the crush of children bore them along in an unstoppable tide toward the eating hall. The rough material chafed her fingers and Mae walked carelessly, sometimes bumping Bincy up against the wall, but Bincy refused to let go. She gazed at Mae's hand, swinging by her side as she walked. She wanted so much to slip her small hand into Mae's and feel the reassuring pressure of fingers curled around her own, but she was too scared.

"Why are you still letting that little thing hang around you? It's been weeks that you've tolerated her now," said one of Mae's friends, Edith.

There was a large ring of them surrounding Mae; all older girls, and all wearing the same tough face as Mae had. Bincy told herself that she felt safe in the center of the circle, but some of them still gave her the same harsh look that Edith wore now.

"Oh, you know how Mrs. Price says we should help the little ones," said Mae, patting the top of Bincy's head. Her singsong voice prompted a wave of laughter from the others in the circle, and Bincy clung to her skirt a little more tightly.

They reached the eating hall. It had seemed so empty the day that Bincy had arrived a few weeks ago, but now, as the flood of girls spilled into the room, it was full almost to bursting. Bincy shot a glance at the gaggle of smallest children, who immediately hurried into a corner and waited there, wide-eyed.

Mae and her friends marched right past them, sometimes pushing them or stepping on their toes as they made their way to the table right at the front, nearest to the tables where the hot bowls of breakfast gruel had been set out ready for them. Bincy shuddered, staying close to Mae. She didn't want to be one of those rejected little children who had to wait until Mae and the others had gotten their food before they were allowed to squabble over the leftovers.

"Stand there," Mae ordered Bincy, pulling her hand away from her skirt. She took her seat at the table, and the other girls followed suit.

"But Mae, you don't have anything to eat yet," said Bincy, casting a longing glance toward the tables.

Mae leaned back in her chair. Her golden locks tumbled freely around her face as she gave Bincy a long, cold look. "Then I suppose you'd better do something about it, don't you think?"

Bincy stared at her, uncomprehending. Mae rolled her eyes, sighing dramatically.

"Go and get our food, you stupid little thing," she said, pointing angrily at the bowls lined up on the table. "And don't dawdle. We don't have all day."

"Oh!" Bincy almost curtsied in relief as she understood. "Of course, Mae."

She hurried off, feeling glad that she could be useful to her new friend. As quick as she could, she brought the bowls two by two to Mae's friends. It took her several trips, and the hot bowls scalded her hands.

"Bincy, what are you doing?" demanded Mrs. Price as Bincy came back for her fifth trip to Mae's friends.

"Just helping my friends, ma'am," said Bincy politely, keeping her eyes down on the table.

"What do you—" Mrs. Price began.

There was a loud crash from the other end of the table. Bincy flinched, and Mrs. Price whipped around.

"Oh, Faye!" she cried in dismay, gazing at the small girl who stood next to a blob of gruel lying on the floor among shattered bits of bowl. "What am I to do with you?"

She bustled toward the crying little girl, and Bincy hurried back to the table with the two bowls. She set the last one down in front of June, the girl who had pushed her off the bunk bed on her first night, and then took her place at the very end of the table.

The gruel was gray and tasteless, but it was warm, and when it slid down Bincy's throat and into her shrunken stomach, it felt good. She choked down three quick bites before Mae spoke. "Hey, Bincy!"

Bincy looked up, her spoon still in her mouth.

"I've finished mine," said Mae. "And I'm much bigger than you. Give me some of yours, won't you?"

"Of course." Bincy jumped up and scrambled over to Mae, spooning some of her gruel over into Mae's bowl.

"Me too," said Edith, holding out her own bowl, even though it was still half full. Bincy obediently did as she was asked. She looked down into her bowl and saw that less than a third of her gruel was left.

Mae glanced carelessly at it and sniffed. "That's quite enough for a scrap like you," she said. "Go and sit at the end of the table, there's a good girl."

Bincy walked away, feeling her heart aching. Mae laughed behind her. "See, Edith?" she said. "She's a useful little thing, really."

Edith's laugh was mean. "I can see why you keep her around."

Bincy took her place at the end of the table again, slowly spooning the gruel into her mouth to make it last as long as she could. She knew that nobody could see the tears that dripped from her cheeks into the gray sludge of her breakfast.

⁂

Bincy stared up at the blackboard at the front of the dreary little classroom. She swung her legs to and fro under her little desk, resisting the urge to slide closer to where Mae sat beside her, even though the cold room made her want to cuddle up as close as she could to the older girl.

"There you go, girls," said their teacher, a weary-eyed lady whose body looked young even though her face was downtrodden by years of struggle. She slumped down by her own desk. "Copy those letters on your slates. When you're done, put up your hand so that I can check your work."

Bincy pulled her heavy slate a little closer, lifting the slate pencil. It still felt awkward and unfamiliar in her hand. She stared hard at the letters on the blackboard, trying to make them make sense. Biting her lip with effort, Bincy bent over her slate and painstakingly copied the shape of the first letter: *A*. She looked back up at the blackboard and felt a bloom of pride. It looked just right.

Looking toward Mae, Bincy held up her slate, wanting to

show her friend how well she'd copied down the letter. She froze halfway through the movement. Mae's slate was blank except for a few nonsensical scrawls and doodles. Instead of looking at the blackboard, the older girl leaned on her desk, looking over at June; they were communicating in a series of gestures, but Bincy could easily understand them. They were making fun of the teacher's skinny frame, laughing silently and pulling faces behind her back every time she turned around to look at the blackboard or engrossed herself in the book on her desk.

Slowly, Bincy put her slate back down again. The soft click as it met the desk caught Mae's attention. She leaned back, staring at Bincy in disdain.

"Won't you look at that," she said, her voice dripping with sarcasm. "Bincy made the most perfect little *A*." Before Bincy could stop her, Mae snatched up the slate, showing it to her friends. "Isn't she just the most perfect little thing?" she hissed. "What pretty, perfect handwriting little Bincy has."

Bincy felt herself blushing. Mae tossed the slate back onto her desk with a clank. The teacher looked up, her eyes severe.

"Bincy Hall," she said sternly.

Bincy cowered in her chair.

"Silence in the class," the teacher ordered. "Don't disrespect the other students by causing a distraction."

"Y-yes, miss," Bincy whispered. "Sorry, miss."

Mae gave a low chuckle that only Bincy and her buddies heard. As soon as the teacher looked down at the book on the desk again, Mae reached over and grabbed Bincy's arm, hard.

"You won't get anywhere around here with your perfect little letters," she hissed.

Bincy whimpered.

"You'd better be sorry." Mae sat back in her chair. "Now, give me your slate. I've drawn all over mine. Take my slate and clear it."

Meekly, Bincy handed over her slate, and Mae started to doodle carelessly on it as Bincy slowly wiped the scribbles from Mae's. She had just finished scrubbing away every last careless scrawl when the big bell rang, and the children started to scramble to their feet for lunch. Bincy quickly put Mae's cleaned slate down on her desk, but Mae leaned over, grabbed it, and switched it for Bincy's slate, which was now covered in doodles. Bincy's heart sank. Now the teacher would think that she was the one doing all that doodling.

It was too late to worry about that now. Mae and her friends were heading for the door, with the other girls hanging back and watching wide-eyed, not daring to get in their way. Bincy ran to catch up with Mae and grabbed hold of her skirt, hanging onto it for dear life as they walked toward the eating hall.

When they entered the hall, Mae and her friends' chatter

bounced and echoed around the empty room. It was made all the emptier by the single, tiny figure that sat at the big table – Mae's table – all by herself. Her eyes were wide, and Mrs. Price stood beside her, watching sternly as the girls filed into the hall.

Bincy wanted to hang back, but Mae didn't hesitate. She marched straight up to the front table, looking at the little girl in disgust. "Who's this, Mrs. Price?" she asked.

Mrs. Price gave Mae a warning look. "This is Catherine," she said, laying a hand on the little girl's shoulder. She couldn't have been any older than Bincy. "She's come to stay with us now."

The warning in Mrs. Price's tone forced Mae to give a simpering smile.

"Ah, how nice to have a new friend," Mae said, her tone falsely sweet. Mrs. Price gave her another warning look, then turned away.

"Lunch will be served in a few minutes. Take your places, girls," she ordered, and marched out toward the kitchens.

The moment the door closed behind Mrs. Price, Mae swung around, turning on the newcomer. "Hello, Catherine," she said savagely. "So what's your story? Did your papa desert you just like Bincy's did?"

Catherine's eyes filled with tears. "No," she whimpered. "My papa is dead. My mama is dead, too. It was the pox that killed them, and now I'm all alone." She pushed her little fists into her eyes and began to sob wholeheartedly.

Bincy wanted to hug her. But Mae grabbed the girl's shoulder, yanking her cruelly to her feet. "I don't care, Catherine," she snarled at the startled child. "All I care about is that you're sitting in my place. Go away."

Releasing Catherine, Mae gave her a little push. "Go," she ordered.

Wide-eyed and still sniveling, Catherine bolted, heading toward one of the other tables where the small children sat. Bincy watched as they silently made space for her, none of them greeting her or daring to offer a few words of comfort as she sat on the cold bench and sniffled with her tears.

Bincy felt a little sick as she took her own place beside Mae, watching the other small children shoot her angry glances. What else could she do? At least if she was close to Mae, she wasn't alone. And all those children sitting there looked terribly alone.

"What are you just sitting here for?" Mae demanded of Bincy. "Go get our lunch."

Bincy mutely began her usual trips up and down, fetching the bowls of watery soup for Mae and her cronies. As she returned from her last trip, Mae leaned over and spoke to Edith. "I think we should welcome our little newcomer properly," she said, a mean glint in her eye. "Don't you?"

Edith grinned, slurping a mouthful of soup. "That sounds good," she said. "What do you have in mind?"

"I guess she'll be in the dormitory next to ours," said Mae. "The only open bed is in there. What do you say we give her a nice cold first night here?"

Edith laughed. "And keep her covers for ourselves so that we have some extra warmth."

"I think it's a good idea," said Mae, laughing cruelly. She looked sideways at Bincy, and her grin widened. "And I know just who should do it so we don't get into trouble."

Bincy stared at her. "What do you want me to do?" she whispered.

"You don't speak unless you're told to," Mae snapped at her. "Sit down."

Meekly, Bincy took her place beside Mae.

"Now, listen closely," said Mae. "Tonight, while we're finishing our dinner, you're going to pretend to be sick and excuse yourself. You'll go to the dormitories and take all of the bedclothes off one of the bunks in the room next to ours and put them on my bed. Understand?"

Bincy stared at Mae in mute horror. It had been so recently that she'd cried herself to sleep on her first night here. How much worse would it have been without even blankets to keep herself warm?

"Do you have a problem with that, Bincy?" Mae asked, her eyes flashing.

Bincy knew better than to argue with Mae. She hung her head. "No, Mae."

"That's a good girl," said Mae, smirking.

BINCY DIDN'T FEEL LIKE A GOOD GIRL AT ALL.

She lay awake in the dark, staring up at the slats of the top bunk where June was snoring loudly. All of the older girls were sleeping peacefully, but their snores and deep breaths couldn't quite drown out the sound that came from the room next door. It was a gentle crying, soft and constant, the kind of continuous sobbing that could go on unabated for hours – for years even. It was the weeping of someone who had lost everything in a day, whose entire world had been turned inside out, who had been catapulted out of one life and into another and found the new life altogether cruel. It was the sound of someone who realized they were completely and utterly alone in a universe that hated them.

It was the sound Bincy thought her heart would make, if she allowed it to. She rolled over, buried her face in her own pillow, and cried along with Catherine.

CHAPTER 4

Four Years Later

"Bincy. Pssst! Bincy, are you awake?"

Bincy opened her eyes. Mae was leaning out of her bunk across from Bincy's, and her eyes were sparkling. "Do you hear that?" she whispered.

"What?" asked Bincy.

"Shhh," said Mae. "Listen."

Bincy turned her head, and after a few moments, she heard it. A soft sobbing, coming from just outside her dormitory. Instantly, she was transported back in time to four years ago, during the first few months of her time in the orphanage. The night she'd heard Catherine crying herself to sleep. Even though she'd since told herself that the night hadn't been her fault, Bincy still felt sick to her stomach as she remembered it. She knew everything she'd done in the past four years had been necessary to survive. Yet there were still things that didn't sit well with her.

"Let's go out and shut that little one up," said Mae, jumping out of bed. "She needs to learn who's the boss around here – and that you don't annoy the boss with your sniveling."

Reluctantly, Bincy dragged herself out of bed and followed Mae to the door. Cracking it open, they spotted one of the new arrivals curled up on the floor in front of her dormitory's door. She couldn't have been much bigger than Bincy was when she first arrived at the orphanage, and when she saw Mae and Bincy standing there, her crying stopped. She stared up at them, silent and wide-eyed.

"What's the matter, little one?" Mae asked in a singsong voice.

The little girl's eyes filled with tears again. "I miss my papa," she said. "I never had no mama, but I miss my papa so much. They put him in jail. Why can't I go and see him?"

Bincy's heart went out to the little girl, but Mae's tone was hard. "Because your papa is a criminal," she snapped. "He's a bad man who did bad things, and he deserves to be in jail."

"He doesn't!" cried the little girl. "He only did it to bring me food. And I was so, so hungry."

Mae laughed. "So he got himself into jail trying to care for you? Then he's stupid as well as a criminal. Who would want to get themselves into trouble for a silly little thing like you?"

"My papa is not stupid!" The little girl jumped to her feet, clenching her fists. "My papa loves me!"

Mae laughed. "Who could ever love you, crying like a little baby out here in the hallway?"

The little girl's cheeks flushed with emotion. She spun around, pushed open the door and rushed into her dormitory, slamming the door loudly behind her. There was an outburst of protest from within the room, and Bincy knew she'd instantly made herself unpopular with everyone she was bunking with.

Mae laughed heartlessly. "That'll teach her," she said. "Come on, Bincy. Let's go and get breakfast."

As Bincy and the other girls sat at breakfast, she kept half an eye on the little one who had been crying in the hallway earlier. She was sitting alone, well away from the others, but unlike most unhappy kids, she didn't push her food around in her plate. Instead, she wolfed it down, gulping at the hard bread and cheese as if it was the first time she'd seen food for a long time. Making sure the other girls in her circle weren't watching, Bincy started slipping scraps of her breakfast into the pockets of her dress.

"I hope Miss Potts is still sick so we don't have to go to

lessons again today," said Mae. "She's only gotten more boring with time."

"Mae," said Bincy, "what if she's really sick?"

"So?" Mae shrugged. "Then we don't have to sit through more of her lessons."

"Bincy's right," said Edith. "If we get someone other than her, they might be even worse."

"Also true," conceded Mae. "Still, I don't see why we have to do lessons at all. Like my mama always said, we're never going to amount to anything anyway. I guess that's why our parents abandoned us."

Bincy didn't want to think of the day that her own mama left her behind in the marketplace. She sneaked a glance up at the little new girl again. Her food was finished, and she was staring down at her empty plate as if she wasn't anywhere close to full.

The bell rang again, signifying breakfast time was over. Mae and the others got to their feet. Bincy followed more slowly, forcing a smile. "I'll catch right up to you," she told them. "I need to run to the bathroom."

"Make it quick," said Mae. "I've got an idea for how we can get Miss Potts back for being boring if she does come to give us lessons today – but we'll have to get to the classroom before she does."

Bincy didn't even want to know what Mae had cooked up for Miss Potts. She headed toward the bathrooms, but as soon as she was out of the eating hall, she waited around the corner until she heard Mae's loud voice receding into the hallway toward the classroom. Moving quickly, Bincy hurried back into the eating hall, but instead of moving toward the classrooms, she spotted the new little girl still sitting by the table as she waited for the others to move out.

She was a fast learner, then. Maybe she could survive here. Bincy hurried over to her. "Hey, little one."

The girl startled, jumping up from her bench. Her pose was defensive, and she said nothing, fixing suspicious eyes on Bincy.

"It's all right." Bincy knelt down, reaching into her pocket. She pulled out her bits of bread and cheese from breakfast and held them out to the little girl. "Here, take these."

Still looking suspicious, the little girl grabbed the food quickly. She pushed the cheese into her mouth and devoured it in one ravenous gulp, then looked up at Bincy again, clutching the bread tightly in her hands. "What do you want? Why are you being nice to me now?"

Bincy ignored the question. "Can I give you one piece of advice?"

The little girl's glare was still suspicious. She nodded, taking a huge bite out of the bread.

"Make friends with someone," said Bincy. "No matter what you have to do. No matter how little you like them. Just find someone who you can be with in this place, or you'll never survive." She gazed sadly toward the hallway where Mae and her friends had headed. "Nothing is ever worse than being all alone."

Before the little girl could answer, Bincy straightened up and hurried away. She had to catch up with Mae as quickly as she could – they had a plot against Miss Potts that needed to be put into action.

"Did you see that little girl wet herself in class this morning?" said Mae, laughing with her mouth full. "It was the most pathetic thing I've ever seen in my life."

"Yes, I saw," said Edith, spluttering. "How old does she think she is, two? They should send her to the workhouse to drink pap like the other orphan babies."

The other girls laughed cruelly. Bincy forced herself to join in with their laughter, but her heart had broken for the little girl when the teacher shouted at her and threatened to cane her for talking loudly in class. Part of her wondered why the teacher didn't do the same to Mae.

"So, what do you think, Mae," said Edith. "Are we finally going to learn to read so we can go to another class?" Her voice was sarcastic, singsong.

"Of course not," said Mae, laughing. "We'll stay right where we are with Miss Potts, who is always too tired and pathetic to notice that we haven't learned anything in years." She bent her back mockingly, mimicking Miss Potts with a high, shaky voice. "'Oooh, my poor back. Oooh, my lungs. Oooh, I'm a young woman but I already have one foot in the grave – and most of my eyesight, too.'"

"'Oooh, I'm so deaf,'" Bincy joined in, adopting the same high voice. The girls laughed uproariously, and Mae slapped her on the back. "You're not so bad, you know, Bincy," she said. "I thought you were a real runt when you first came here, but you've turned out all right."

Bincy felt a warm glow seep through her. She grinned, enjoying the attention. "I knew I'd be all right as long as I stayed with you, Mae," she said loyally.

"Of course, you will," said Mae, tossing an arm carelessly around Bincy's shoulders. "I'll look out for you."

Mae's touch was callous, but it was the only time anyone ever gave her anything like affection, and Bincy craved it. She leaned against her friend for a moment before pulling away. She didn't want to make Mae angry.

"Silence, please." Mrs. Price's voice rang out across the eating hall, and it held a solemnity so powerful that the entire hall quietened instantly. Every head in the hall turned to stare at her. Mrs. Price was standing at the front table, and her expression was as grave as a gray stone in a cemetery. She studied the girls for a long, icy moment, and her eyes came to rest on Bincy. Their stern and cold expression struck terror straight into the marrow of her bones.

"I have a very grim announcement to make," Mrs. Price said.

Bincy's heart almost stopped. The only other time she'd ever heard Mrs. Price use those words had been when one of the girls had died in her sleep. She reached for Mae's hand instinctively, but Mae yanked it away.

"We have done everything in our power at this orphanage to be able to provide for you children," said Mrs. Price. Her eyes were steely, and she was still looking at Bincy. "Sometimes this requires great personal sacrifice, sometimes not, but it's always a huge task. And I believe we do our best to make sure you all go to bed with full stomachs at night." Mrs. Price leaned forward. "That is why what I'm about to tell you is so very grave. Someone has been stealing food from the kitchen. We only just have enough for all of you, and if someone takes food, there won't be enough for the rest of you." Her mouth was grimly set. "Half a bread pudding was stolen last night."

Bincy's stomach twisted. Who would do such a thing? Mrs. Price was grim and scary, but Bincy knew that without her, she would have starved to death – either on the streets or in some bleak warehouse. She couldn't imagine taking anything from her.

"Ordinarily, you would all be punished with extra chores and have your pudding taken away," said Mrs. Price. "But this time, there is no need. I know exactly who has done this, and I plan to make an example of her." Mrs. Price raised her chin, her eyes still fixed on Bincy. "Bincy Hall."

"What?" Bincy gasped as a murmur ran through the entire eating hall. Her blood felt cold in her veins.

"Miss Hall." Mrs. Price picked up her walking cane into both hands. "Come here."

Bincy's stomach churned. She had never felt the cane before; she'd never had reason to be punished. "I-I didn't do it, Mrs. Price," she said. "I would never steal from you. I'd never do such a thing."

Mrs. Price's eyes flashed. "Are you calling me a liar, Miss Hall?"

"No! No, ma'am," stammered Bincy. "There has to be some mistake. I didn't take the pudding, I promise." She turned to Mae and her friends. "Please, Mae. Tell her. I wouldn't do it."

Mae's sympathetic expression was as false as her sweet tone. She shrugged. "I don't know what you're capable of, Bincy."

Bincy stared at her, and in that moment, she was seven years old again and screaming for her mother as the policeman held her back. The pain, the confusion – it all came flooding right back again with a force that took her breath away. She couldn't move, couldn't speak, couldn't even look up. She just stared at Mae.

"Miss Hall." Mrs. Price's voice was as final as a closing coffin. "Come up here. I will not ask you again."

As in a fog, Bincy rose to her feet. She almost staggered over to Mrs. Price, feeling the blood rushing in her veins. Her legs seemed to be carrying her of their own accord, irresistibly drawn by the ice in Mrs. Price's eyes. As soon as she reached the old woman, Mrs. Price laid a hand on her shoulder – or not so much a hand as a cold, steel claw.

"I thought better of you than this, Bincy," she said softly, her eyes filled with disappointment. "But when we found that bread pudding hidden underneath your bed, I couldn't ignore the evidence."

Bincy couldn't formulate an argument. All she stammered out was, "Please."

"I'm sorry," said Mrs. Price, looking away. "But I have to make an example of you. I cannot tolerate this behavior in my orphanage. Turn around and pull up your skirts to bare your calves."

Bincy did as she was told. The first crack of the cane across her bare skin was painful; the second, on the same bruised spot, was agonizing. By the third and fourth, she was crying openly, and she could hear the muted giggles from the eating hall. Pain and humiliation streamed through her as the cane thwacked down time and time again on her bare calves until she could feel lines of fire sketched across her skin. She lost count of the blows by the time Mrs. Price finally stopped, breathing heavily.

For a moment, there was no sound except for Bincy's soft sniffing. She stared down at the floor, which was spotted with tears.

"This is what will happen to you if you take from us, when we've done so much to provide for you," said Mrs. Price heavily. "Now, Miss Hall, you will come with me."

Bincy looked up, frightened. "Where are we going?"

"Be quiet," said Mrs. Price. She grabbed Bincy's arm in an iron fist. "Let's go."

Bincy's skirt chafed across her bruised calves as she was more or less dragged out of the eating hall. Almost paralyzed with terror, she had little option other than to allow herself to stagger along behind Mrs. Price, who was walking very fast with her back very straight. They headed through the dormitories and into a part of the orphanage that Bincy hadn't seen before. She glimpsed an office, and then they reached a narrow door that led to a tiny, windowless room. There was a pallet on the floor, and everything was covered in a layer of dust.

"I haven't had to use this room much before," said Mrs. Price, her voice laced with sorrow. "I had hoped I would never have to use it again." She gave Bincy a shove, pushing her into the room.

"What is this place?" gasped Bincy, spinning around to look at Mrs. Price.

The ice had melted out of the old woman's eyes, leaving an aching sorrow. "This is the refractory ward," she said simply. "Your meals will be brought to you. You will stay in here for three days."

Bincy was shaking all over. "Alone?"

"Yes," said Mrs. Price. "Alone. Use this time to think about what you've done."

She stepped back, and Bincy rushed forward. "Mrs. Price, no! Please!"

It was too late. The door slammed, and Bincy fell against it, screaming as the walls of the tiny room started to close in around her. "NO! PLEASE! MRS. PRICE!" she shrieked at the top of her lungs. "Let me out! I didn't do it! I said I DIDN'T DO IT!"

But she may as well have been screaming to the walls for all the good it did. She collapsed slowly, wrapping her arms around herself, sobbing uncontrollably. The world had never felt colder. Her heart had never felt emptier.

The refractory ward seemed to bend the very concept of time. Meals came and went; so did light, but Bincy mostly lay curled on her pallet, cold and scared and inexpressibly alone. It was as if the outside world had been wiped away completely. She couldn't make herself believe that just a brick's width away, there was color and light and sound and people and talking. Here, there was nothing. Just whitewashed walls and a silence that echoed to the very core of her being.

A point came when she couldn't cry or panic anymore; not because she'd grown used to the walls that felt like they were falling in on her, but because she was too exhausted even to sleep. She just lay on her pallet, her head resting on her arm, letting her feelings have their way with her. The same moment kept coming back into her mind over and over: her last moment with Mama, and the disappointment in her eyes.

After the first three meals, she began to eat, but there was no appetite or flavor in the eating; it was almost mechanical, a purely biological necessity. She couldn't tell if she'd been in the cell for two days or two years. It felt like centuries.

Finally, there was a creak, and the door opened. Bincy looked up immediately, even though she was still eating her breakfast. Every time someone came in, she gazed at them as if they were the only thing in her whole world, despite the fact that they were normally just one of the two dour-faced maids.

Today, though, it was Mrs. Price. Previously, Bincy would have recoiled from her in fear. This time, she just stared at her, drinking in the wonder of a human presence.

Mrs. Price's expression was gentle with sorrow. She held out her hand. "Come, Bincy," she said. "I think you've had enough."

Bincy jumped to her feet, pushing her plate away onto the pallet. "R-really?" she gasped.

"Yes. Come," said Mrs. Price.

Bincy wanted to run out of that room as fast as her legs could carry her. Instead, she forced herself to take small steps, following Mrs. Price as closely as she dared. The moment she stepped into the hallway, it felt as though she was breathing out for the first time in days. Now everything was going to be normal again. She could go back to lessons and eating and sleeping in the dormitory with Mae and her other friends, and everything would be all right again.

She expected Mrs. Price to take her straight to the classroom, but instead, the older woman seemed to be heading toward the eating hall. Bincy decided it was wisest not to ask any questions. She followed her down the hallway and into the cavernous hall, which was empty except for stacks of dirty dishes.

"Where... where is everyone?" Bincy said at last, almost whispering in fear.

"At lessons," said Mrs. Price curtly.

Bincy was too afraid to ask why she wasn't being taken to lessons, too. She found herself in a hallway that she'd barely seen since coming to the orphanage: the one leading to the outside, to the front door where the kindly policeman had left her. Had something changed when she was locked up? Where were Mae and the others?

Mrs. Price didn't turn off into any of the doorways lining the hall. Instead, she got to the front door and pulled it wide open.

For the first time in four years, Bincy set eyes on the street outside. She was frozen, her feet rooted to the ground as she stared out at it. She had forgotten that the outside world could be so huge, that there was anything in existence as massive as the gray sky above them, heavy with the promise of rain. Somehow it seemed to be so much bigger than it was in the yard at the back of the building where the girls went during recess. Its size was dizzying, terrifying; it felt like it might suck her in and crush her, and she couldn't decide which was worse – the open sky or the clinging walls of the cell.

Mrs. Price was standing impatiently in the doorway. "Come on," she said. "We're leaving."

Her words made no sense. Bincy stared at her blankly. "Leaving?" she said.

"Yes, leaving," said Mrs. Price. Bincy couldn't tell if it was disappointment, sadness or anger in her eyes. "I don't have all day. Come on."

Bincy took a step back. "I-I don't understand."

"Don't make this harder than it already is, Bincy," said Mrs. Price. "I don't want to do this any more than you want me to do this, but there's no other way. I can't trust you, and I can't allow your bad influence to teach the other girls to steal." She sighed heavily. "A family came to me asking if I had someone who could be a scullery maid for them. It's the only way."

"N-no." Bincy's heart hammered. She stepped back again, her thoughts flying to Mae. "I can't go there alone. I can't go without Mae."

"Bincy, stop," said Mrs. Price, coming back into the hallway. "Come back here."

"No!" Bincy backed away, hearing the shriek in her own voice. "No, I can't, I can't, I can't!"

Mrs. Price seized her arm. "Don't be a fool, girl," she snapped. "This is only making it harder for yourself."

Someone needed to help her. Bincy knew that Mae had stolen that bread pudding and that she'd been betrayed, but there was no one else in the whole world she could think of to help her.

"MAE!" she screamed at the top of her lungs. "MAE!"

"Be quiet!" snapped Mrs. Price. She pulled hard on Bincy's arm, yanking her bodily toward the doorway.

"Maaaaaaae!" screamed Bincy, as loudly as she could.

She couldn't resist Mrs. Price. The older woman was as strong as she was severe, and she found herself being dragged out of the doorway. "NO! Let me go! MAE, HELP ME!" Bincy shrieked.

Mrs. Price's ringing slap across her face came as a shock. Immediately, Bincy went silent. She stared at Mrs. Price, feeling pain blossom across her cheek.

"That's enough," said Mrs. Price. "We're going, and that's final." Her fist on Bincy's arm was an iron shackle. "Now walk with me, or I will send you to the workhouse."

Tears poured down Bincy's cheeks as she followed Mrs. Price meekly out onto the street and walked along the pavement with her, feeling her heart pounding. She wanted to scream again, but she didn't. She wasn't afraid of another slap from Mrs. Price.

She knew nobody was ever going to come to save her.

PART II

CHAPTER 5

Bincy's legs were aching. She had never seen this part of the city before; her memories were all of cold, gray buildings and filthy slums, but this place was completely different. She didn't know there were places like this in the whole world. Here, the street was swept cleaner than the floors of the orphanage. There were trees growing here, not the sorry, naked things that stood guard on the street corners of the slum, but towering pillars of growing life. The buildings had fences around them and intact windows, and even long lawns so green that Bincy could hardly believe they were natural.

Mrs. Price was walking more slowly now, too, and Bincy had a chance to gaze open-mouthed at the massive buildings lining the street. She couldn't tell what they were. They were as big as the orphanage had been, but without its sternness; perhaps, they were some kind of fancier tenement, she thought.

They reached a street corner, and Mrs. Price looked down at the slip of paper in her hand. She squinted at the number on the gate of the nearest building.

"Almost there, Bincy," she said, sounding relieved.

Bincy didn't dare ask where they were going. She followed silently as Mrs. Price led her to one of the buildings further down the street. This one had towering pine trees lining a gravel driveway that led up to its elegant front; there was a lawn on either side of the driveway, and it split to accommodate a fountain at its center, where a gentle cascade of water spilled over a statue of an angel kneeling with its face up to heaven.

Instead of walking up to the door by the fountain, Mrs. Price led Bincy around the edge of the lawn. It seemed to take ages to walk around to the back of the huge building; they passed gardens and a huge stable block that smelled like Bincy's straw mattress back in the orphanage. Finally, they reached a small door set deep in the back of a part of the building that had little windows and a neglected air about it.

Mrs. Price knocked on the door. Bincy couldn't contain her fear any longer. "Mrs. Price?" she croaked.

"Yes, child?" Mrs. Price's voice was resigned.

"What is this place?"

Mrs. Price looked down, surprised. "Why, this is a manor house, of course."

"A house?" Bincy gaped at it. "So only one family lives here?"

"Yes. Well – a family and their servants, in any case. You're one of them now."

Bincy didn't know what to think. Then, the door opened, and a large woman with enormously bushy black eyebrows glared down at her. She wanted to hide behind Mrs. Price.

"Is this the girl?" the woman asked bluntly.

"Yes, this is Bincy Hall," said Mrs. Price. "Your new scullery-maid." Mrs. Price turned to Bincy. "This is Mrs. Davids, the housekeeper here. You are to listen to everything she tells you."

The woman glared at Bincy. "Scrawny little mite, isn't she? Are you sure she can do the work? She looks sickly."

"She was when she came to us, but if she gets enough to eat, she's surprisingly strong," said Mrs. Price.

"Hmm." Mrs. Davids studied Bincy for a few seconds longer. "Better than nothing, I suppose. You've been paid, haven't you?"

"Yes, I have," said Mrs. Price. "Thank you."

She pushed Bincy forward toward Mrs. Davids, forcing her to stagger a few reluctant steps. Mrs. Price's hand stayed on her shoulder for a moment, and when Bincy looked up at her, she thought she might have seen a tear glimmering in Mrs. Price's eyes.

"Be a good girl," said Mrs. Price thickly.

Then she was gone, and Bincy was alone with Mrs. Davids. She stared up at her, feeling herself tremble. Mrs. Davids seemed to be less a human being than she was a towering monument of suppressed wrath. Giving Bincy another glare, Mrs. Davids shook the doorknob impatiently. "Are you going to stand there all day, girl? Get in here."

"Y-yes, ma'am," Bincy squeaked. She scurried inside, and the door closed firmly behind her, sealing them off in the twilight of the great building.

Bincy stared around her. She was inside a kitchen just as big as the one back at the orphanage, but instead of the pervading smell of porridge and boiling gruel, this one was filled with a delicious scent Bincy didn't recognize. She wondered if this was roast beef, which one of the other girls had told her about before. Hooks suspended from the ceiling held hams; there were tureens of fresh, colorful vegetables on the great table that stood in the center of the room, and three pots were bubbling on the stove, fragrant steam rising from their surfaces. Not a tin cup was in sight – instead, piles of China plates stood on the shelves above the stove.

"What are you standing there for?" demanded Mrs. Davids. "I told you to come with me."

"Yes, ma'am. Sorry, ma'am," Bincy stammered out. She followed Mrs. Davids at a jog as they moved through the kitchen.

THE FORSAKEN MAID'S SECRET

"The cellar is that way," said Mrs. Davids, pointing to a door on their left. "And this is the scullery, where you'll be doing most of your work."

She pushed open another door, leading Bincy into a gray room that smelled of dirty dishes. The light inside was as bare, cold, and severe as Mrs. Davids' manner; but nothing could hold more naked chill than the eyes of the girl who stood by one of the vast sinks set against the wall. She wiped her hands on a dishcloth as Mrs. Davids and Bincy approached. Her eyes flashed like two pieces of ice in her skull.

"Is this the new scullery maid, ma'am?" she asked, her voice polite, her eyes disdainful.

"Yes, it is. Try not to cause this one to run away in six months, would you?" said Mrs. Davids. She gave Bincy a push in the girl's direction. "It's expensive to keep finding new ones."

The girl laughed. "As you wish, ma'am," she said mockingly.

"Watch your tone, Ada." Mrs. Davids gave her a flat glare. "You'd do well to remember that you're only a kitchen maid yourself."

"Of course, ma'am," said Ada sweetly.

Mrs. Davids gave her a last, suspicious look before walking away. Bincy would have run if she'd known which direction would be safest. Instead, she just stared up at Ada, wide-eyed and trembling.

Ada came a few steps nearer. She folded her arms, glaring down at Bincy. "Do you know why you're here?"

"Yes, miss," whispered Bincy. "They think I stole the bread pudding, but it was Mae actually. So..."

"Wrong," said Ada. Bincy blinked at her in surprise as the older girl went on. "You're here to be a scullery maid. I was a scullery maid too, once, so I know exactly what it's all about. Do you know what being a scullery maid means?"

Bincy shook her head, too scared to speak.

"It means that you do everything the kitchen maid tells you to do," said Ada. "Whatever the kitchen maid says, that's what you do, no matter how miserable it is or how long you have to spend working." She grinned, a wolfish expression that made Bincy take a step back in fear. "And do you know who the kitchen maid is around here?"

Bincy swallowed. She didn't ask. She didn't have to.

"I am," said Ada, relishing Bincy's fear. "That means you have to do exactly what I tell you to do. Understand?" She turned away, laughing. "And the first thing I'm going to tell you to do is to wash those dishes."

Bincy followed Ada's pointing finger to the sink. It was enormous – so big that Bincy could comfortably have used it for a bath – and stacked with delicate China dishes. Bincy couldn't believe the sheer number of them. There were enough to feed the entire orphanage and then some.

"All of them?" Bincy whispered.

Ada laughed. "Yes, all of them," she said. "Don't move until you're done." She flounced away and slammed the door, leaving Bincy all alone with only her sadness and a great sink full of empty dishes for company.

Bincy didn't know what to do with sadness. But like all the other girls, she'd had a turn to help in the kitchen at the orphanage, so at least she knew what to do about dishes. Hesitantly, she made her way over to the sink and plunged her hands into the greasy water. It didn't feel like she had much of a choice, so she took the first dish and began to wash, allowing her tears to drip down into the water so that it looked as though they had never been cried.

CHAPTER 6

It felt to Bincy as though there was simply no end to the dishes. One by one, she sponged the sticky food from them, rinsed them clean, and packed them into the enormous drying rack that stood down the length of one wall of the scullery. At first, pushing her hands into the murky dish water was disgusting; but after the first two hours by the clock on the wall, Bincy didn't care anymore. Her hands and arms were sore from the effort when she finally finished. She looked up at the clock. It was afternoon already, and the skin on her hands was whitened and wrinkled, as if she'd aged decades in hours. It certainly felt that way.

"Miss?" Bincy called out, nervous. She peered around the huge table that stood in the middle of the scullery to where Ada was busy polishing the silverware. The kitchen maid looked up, irritated. "I told you to shut up and finish those dishes," she snapped.

"I-I'm done, miss," said Bincy. "They're finished."

Ada sneered at her. "Your work is *never* finished, scullery maid," she snapped.

She was interrupted by the ring of a bell from somewhere deeper into the house. Ada perked up, her expression brightening. "Lunch," she said happily, getting to her feet.

Bincy was starving. The word "lunch" brought a ray of light into her broken heart, and she hurried after Ada as the kitchen maid left the scullery and moved through the kitchen, pushing open a door at the far end. Bincy just caught a glimpse of a hall beyond – a simple wooden table standing down its length, with steaming pots and plates resting upon it – before Ada moved inside and went to close the door.

"Wait!" Bincy gasped, rushing forward.

Ada's eyes flashed fire. "What do you want?" she demanded.

"I-I just th-thought that, p-p-p-perhaps..." Bincy whimpered, wilting in the face of Ada's wrath.

"Oh, you thought you were going to eat here with the rest of the servants?" Ada gave a mocking laugh. "No. Scullery maids don't eat with us. Sit in the kitchen and keep an eye on those pots on the stove – don't let them burn; they're the master's dinner." She flapped a condescending hand toward Bincy. "Find some scraps and eat those for lunch for all I care."

The door slammed. Bincy closed her eyes, trembling with sorrow and hurt. Regardless of what Mae had done, she missed her with everything in her heart. If only Mae was here, at least there would be someone to protect her. Someone who wasn't scared to death of Ada like she was.

※

Bincy was so hungry that even the smell of raw fish rising from the trout she was scaling seemed appetizing. The scales stuck to her fingers, scattering softly across the table where she worked; her hands moved painstakingly – she'd learned the hard way not to damage the skin of the fish and cut into its flesh. Her mouth watered as she thought of how this trout must taste; its smell, once the cook had roasted to it to perfection, was indescribable. Bincy had never tasted something like it before.

She found herself longing to go back to the orphanage and the big bowls of gruel or vegetable soup that she and the other girls had eaten three times a day. It was never tasty, and sometimes it was downright difficult to persuade the tasteless mixtures down her throat, but at least there was always enough to go around – enough so nobody went to bed hungry, at least.

In the past five days, Bincy had gone to bed hungry every

single night. She swallowed, trying to hold back her tears as she thought of her lonely supper the night before. Ada and the others had been in the eating hall, eating offal and potatoes. Bincy's supper had consisted of one cold potato and the heel of the loaf of bread. She couldn't remember when last she'd been this hungry. It must have been right before Mama left her in the marketplace, abandoned her alone in a city so big it threatened to trample her and swallow her whole...

"What are you doing?"

Bincy spun around, frightened. Ada was standing directly behind her, only a foot away, and she looked furious – even more so than usual.

"I'm just s-scaling the fish," Bincy gasped out.

"How can you still be scaling the fish?" Ada demanded. "You were supposed to have finished this hours ago. You should have started on scouring the pots already!"

Tears filled Bincy's eyes. She couldn't help it, but she tried her best to swallow them down. "I'm so sorry," she sobbed. "I'm trying not to cut the skin."

"That's no excuse for taking this long to scale a few trout, you miserable little mite," said Ada scathingly.

"Don't be angry," Bincy whimpered. "I'm sorry. I'm just hungry and I don't feel well and—"

"Do you think I care?" bellowed Ada. "Kitchen maids don't

care about little scullery maids, child. Nobody does. I should know." She was trembling with rage as if she might explode at any minute. Instead, she grabbed Bincy's arm, pinching it cruelly. "Well, if you won't do as you're told, you'll have to learn your lesson."

"Let me go!" Bincy gasped, trying to pull away.

Ada gave her a shake that made Bincy's teeth rattle. "Shut up!" she roared. "You're coming with me, you insolent thing."

She dragged her over to the great cupboard in the back of the scullery, the one where the brooms and mops were kept, and yanked open the door. The interior was dark and riddled with spiderwebs, and it made Bincy's heart flip over.

"N-no!" she gasped, trying to pull back. But her limbs were weak with hunger, and Ada was older and stronger. She forced Bincy into the cupboard and gave her a last sneer. "A few hours in here will teach you a lesson," she snarled, and slammed the door.

The closing door sealed Bincy in perfect darkness. She threw herself against it, her breathing harsh and ragged with fear. A broom fell over beside her, rapping painfully on her shins.

"Please, Ada, let me out!" she gasped. "Please!"

"Every time you scream, I'll add an hour to your time in there," hissed Ada angrily through the door.

The idea was frightening enough that Bincy fell completely

silent. She cowered in the cupboard, her hands trembling uncontrollably. Her mind ran in wild circles, looking for a way out. The cupboard was latched from the outside; she would have to reason with Ada somehow, although she wasn't sure if that was even possible.

"Please, Ada," she said, trying to keep her voice as level as possible. "I-I have so much work. If you lock me in here, I won't get it all done today."

Ada's voice was close, as if she were leaning right up against the keyhole in her glee. "Oh, you don't have to finish your work today," she said, her voice syrup sweet.

Bincy frowned. "Wh-what do you mean?" she asked, not buying Ada's false sweetness.

"You'll scour those pots tonight," said Ada, laughing. "You're not going to bed until all your work is done. Enjoy your time in the cupboard – it's the only rest you'll be getting today." She gave a last, nasty chortle before her footsteps grew quieter and quieter and the scullery door slammed behind her.

BINCY USUALLY HATED THE CACOPHONY OF THE KITCHEN when all the preparations were in full swing. Clashing silverware in the drawers, plates clinking against each other, simmering pots, shouting voices – she found it overwhelming, a chaos all too familiar from spending years living with a large number of other girls. Now, though, the silence was much louder than any noise could ever be.

Bincy splashed the pots around in the cold sink, trying to create some kind of sound to strive against the oppressive quiet, but the silence was like some vengeful animal. It crawled in the shadows from one rafter to another, seeping down all the dark corners and reaching up behind Bincy to squeeze her in a stifling fist that threatened to crush the breath from her lungs. It was so thick that she didn't know what could be hiding in it, and it was as terrifying as it was unfamiliar. Even in the depth of night back at the orphanage, there was always someone snoring or sighing or rolling over on the bunk, a sense of community all around Bincy.

Here, there was just the echoing space of the kitchen, and she would have given anything to have Mae near her. For four years, they had eaten, slept, and gone to class together, never more than a doorway away from each other. Being without her felt like being cut loose from reality somehow. She felt adrift.

The temperature of the water in the sink wasn't helping, either. She was too small to lift the great cast-iron pot from its hook over the fire, so the water she was using was as cold as the wind outside. It made her chapped hands ache at first, then gradually turned them so numb that she could barely hold the pot-scourer as she scrubbed it back and forth across the sticky surface of the pots. The residue of food left in this one had hardened into an almost impenetrable grime. Knowing that cleaning it would have been much easier if she could have done it as soon as she was done with the fish didn't help either. Now, it was well past ten, and Bincy was the only one left awake in the entire house.

There was a thump from somewhere deeper in the kitchen. Bincy froze, staying motionless until even the gentle sloshing of the water in the sink died down. Not a cricket chirped; even the street was empty, and the silence seemed to be crushing her. But surely, she had heard something. She glanced nervously toward the cellar door, but it was securely closed. Somehow, that made it worse. She wished she could see inside.

Swallowing hard, Bincy tried to shake herself mentally. "It's nothing," she whispered to herself, grabbing the scourer again. "You're only imagining things. You'll be done in a jiffy and then you can climb into your nice, warm…"

There was another thump, and this time a tinkle, like breaking glass. Bincy shook her head, splashing more loudly in the water. She was imagining things. She just had to work faster so she could drown out the force of her loneliness. If only Mae could be with her now – even her constant berating would be more welcome than the strange noises Bincy knew couldn't be real.

Was that a footstep? Bincy whirled around, splashing cold water across the floor, holding the pot scourer like a weapon.

But there was no one there; the scullery was as vast and empty as it had been when Ada had finally let her out of the cupboard. Shaking, Bincy turned back to her work. Of course, there was no one there.

There was never anyone there, not when she needed them.

❦

The clock on the wall read twenty past midnight when Bincy was finally finished with the pots. She knew she would have to be up before five to light the fires in the kitchen. Her chest hurt every time she coughed, and she was coughing hard now as she dried her hands on a cloth and stumbled toward the servants' quarters. The hallway was dark, but Bincy was too tired and felt too poorly to care about the blackness that threatened to engulf her. She felt her way to the second door on the left and tiptoed into the room she shared with Ada.

Bincy had almost made it to her pallet on the floor when she could no longer hold in the cough that was trying to claw its way up her throat. It ripped loose, loud and hacking in the darkness, and Bincy dived into her pallet. It was too late. Ada shot upright in bed, her rage almost audible even before she spoke.

"Shut up!" she snapped. "How dare you wake me?" The whites of her eyes gleamed in the scrap of moonlight that found its way between the crack in the curtains. "You're getting another two hours in the cupboard tomorrow, you useless little girl."

Bincy said nothing, even though her heart screamed in pain. She just closed her lips tightly, pulled her rough blanket over her head, and wished with all her heart that she could be back in a dormitory full of girls, in a place where bedtime was always the same and there was dinner for everyone.

CHAPTER 7

The exhaustion dragging at the corners of Bincy's eyes and weighing down her feet somehow made the noises worse.

She had done everything she could to please Ada during the day, even though she felt sick and weak after getting only a few hours of rest. She'd polished the silver without being asked, finished chopping the carrots in record time, taken out the garbage, and even put the water on the coal stove to boil for the cook, though normally the cook did that herself. But none of it had meant anything to Ada. The moment Bincy had accidentally tipped the jug of milk just a little when she set it down on the table, spilling three drops on the wood sent Ada into a rage.

As had become usual over the past few weeks, Bincy spent lunchtime locked up in the cupboard, and now it was half past ten again, and she was still in the kitchen, cleaning the stove as well as she could by the flickering light of the oil lamp on the kitchen table. The lamp made her shadow dance on the wall every time she moved, like some manic beast jumping up to scare her when she straightened up to clean the top of the stove. With the stove empty, the cold was unimaginable. It felt like it was seeping straight into the marrow of her bones.

That was when Bincy heard it again – that noise. The thump from the cellar. She gritted her teeth, knowing she was imagining it. Scrubbing harder, she began to hum, trying to drown it out without waking the other servants. Perhaps, if she believed hard enough that there was nothing there, she would be right. She finished the stove and headed toward the sink full of dishes waiting for her to wash and paused for a moment, listening. This time, she heard a gentle scrape, like someone pulling a heavy item off a shelf. For a moment, she stared at the cellar door. What if she went over there and opened it? Would she see anything?

Or nothing?

And would that be worse than discovering something in there?

Bincy shook herself. She had to get her work done, or she'd never get to bed. When a new fit of coughs bubbled their way up her throat and tore at her body, they were almost welcome. She couldn't hear anything except for her own ragged breaths as she got started on the dishes, plunging her hands into the oily water and rubbing them clean of the congealed food that slid queasily between her fingers.

Another thump. This one was loud – it made Bincy spin around, a plate almost slipping between her fingers. She clutched it, trembling as she listened. It had sounded just like a heavy footstep. She stared at the cellar, unable to face whichever was true: that there really was something in there, or that she was going mad.

The silence became oppressive again, so she turned back to the sink, pushing the plate through the rinse water as quickly as she could. She began to hum one of the hymns she'd learned in the orphanage during their twice daily prayer time. "Glory to Thee, my God, this night," she whispered, her voice hesitantly following the gentle tune. "For all the blessings of the light." Those blessings felt very far away as she placed the dish on the drying rack and reached for another. "Keep me, O keep me, King of kings, beneath Thine own almighty wings."

There was something from the cellar – scratching, almost whispering. Bincy raised her voice for the next verse. "Teach me to live, that I may dread the grave as little as my bed," she gasped. "Teach me to die, so that I may rise glorious..."

Clop. Clop. Clop. Footsteps. This time, they came from the door leading to the servants' quarters. Bincy wheeled around, feeling herself trembling. No. It wasn't real. She was imagining things. She cleared her throat, shaking her way back into the song. "Rise glorious at the... the awful... day..."

The footsteps were upon her now. She couldn't stop shaking as she heard them coming closer and closer, and their ringing purpose terrified her. She took a step back, her shaking breaths rushing through her. Who was going to come through that door?

Or what?

The door slammed open. Bincy gave a little scream and leaped back, throwing up her hands to protect herself. But the monstrosity that came through the door was a familiar one: Ada, and her face was twisted in a caricature of fury.

"What are you doing?" she demanded, her voice ripping through the whole kitchen.

There was a crash from the cellar. Bincy spun, staring at it. That had been real – she knew it.

"Answer me!" Ada thundered, lunging closer. Before Bincy could duck, the kitchen maid had seized her arm and delivered a heavy blow across Bincy's face. She gasped in pain, grasping for words. "J-j-j-j-just singing a h-hymn, Ada," she managed.

"Singing a *hymn*? Do you think that could save you, you little fool?" Ada roared. "You're waking the whole house with your racket!"

"There's something in the cellar," Bincy pleaded. "Please. It's making noises."

Ada's expression was wild with rage. "The only noises here are in your empty little head," she hissed. "And if I hear so much as a peep from you for the rest of the night, I'll see to it that you don't sleep for a week." She gave Bincy a cruel shake. "Understand?"

Bincy lowered her head, hiding her tears. "Yes, miss."

"Good. Now get back to work." Ada pushed her away. "And be quiet about it this time."

Bincy held it together until Ada slammed the kitchen door behind her. Then, she sank slowly to the floor, plastering her hands over her mouth so that nobody could hear the sobs that rose uncontrollably from somewhere deep in her guts and burst in damp profusion into her shaking palms.

It was true, then – she was going mad, because Ada hadn't heard the noises. How long would it be before she heard things during the day, too? She remembered the old men she'd seen on the street as a little girl with her mother. Some of them had gibbered incoherently; others had drool running out of their mouths as they cackled at them. She could hear the noises again now, and her fear of becoming like those men was overwhelming; they were footsteps now, and they were definitely in the cellar, coming toward her.

Would she starve on the streets too, so pathetic that she was beneath even pity, laughing senselessly and gasping gibberish?

The footsteps came to the very door of the cellar and

stopped. Bincy held her breath despite her burning throat. What if that door opened? What would she do if she was seeing things, too? There was a hissing noise, like someone being shushed. Then, the doorknob turned. Bincy stared at it, mesmerized, frozen in her terror. The hinges creaked a little, and the door swung open.

Bincy stared at the two shapes for a moment, her heart beating wildly in her ears, erratic and panicked. There were two of them, and one was a hulking figure, silhouetted by lantern light inside the cellar, its face shrouded in the shadows of the hood over its head. Or maybe it wasn't a hood. Maybe it was some strange creature – a demon or a faerie – and it was coming to get her.

Bincy could no longer control herself. She didn't have the breath to scream. Pop-eyed in silence, she rushed at the monster, desperate to defend herself. The bigger apparition threw up two white claws and croaked in surprise; the smaller one by its side gave a high-pitched little yelp, and then Bincy was upon them, flailing madly with her arms, panting in her panic.

Her hands slapped against something hard and real, like flesh, and Bincy knew a moment of hesitation. Could this thing be human? Then the claws shot out and grasped her wrists, and she gave a gasp of terror and dismay. Hissing, the thing leaned closer to her, its horrible face coming closer, the strange odor of its breath rolling around her. She would have screamed if she hadn't been too scared to breathe. She kicked out, her foot smashing into one of the kitchen shelves nearby; she heard the tinkle of something breaking, and her attacker simply lifted her off the floor by her waving arms, still hissing. Her fear had made her dizzy now. She continued to squirm, panic overwhelming her, gathering her breath for a scream—

"Quiet!" the monster hissed.

Bincy hesitated. Had that been a spoken word?

"It's all right," the creature repeated, lowering her so that her feet touched the ground again. She stood there, trembling, staring at its shadowed face. "Don't be frightened. We're not here to harm you."

Bincy swallowed against her bone-dry mouth. She had to make two attempts before she could get the words out. "What are you?"

"What... Oh!" The bigger creature turned to the small one. "Clara – hurry and bring the light. But be quiet."

A few moments later, the lantern was brought nearer. Bincy summoned her courage and looked up. The thing holding her wasn't a monster; it was a boy, older than her, but still a child himself. His face was pinched and pale, and his eyes a gentle shade of gray, sad as a rainy day. He reached up and pushed back his hood, and Bincy felt herself relaxing. His shaggy brown hair was dirty, but he was no ghost or faerie. Just a human being.

"What are you doing in the cellar?" she managed.

The boy let go of her arms. She backed away, rubbing her wrists where he'd been holding her. "Who are you?" he asked.

"Bincy Hall," said Bincy. "I'm the scullery maid here."

The boy reached out, and the smaller monster – a little girl, Bincy saw, several years younger than herself – took his hand. He drew her close to him as he spoke. "We thought you'd gone out of the kitchen at last," said the boy. "Otherwise, we wouldn't have frightened you." There was both regret and fear in his voice. "Are you going to call the housekeeper?"

Bincy didn't need to think about her answer. "No," she said. Mrs. Davids was terrifying – she wanted to spend as little time as possible anywhere near her.

The boy's shoulders sagged with relief. "Thank you," he said.

"Why are you in this house?" Bincy asked. "Are you thieves?"

The boy looked pained. He sighed, sitting down on a barrel near the doorway of the cellar, and pulled the little girl onto his lap. "I suppose you could say we are," he said reluctantly.

"But you said we weren't," said the little girl, looking up at him. Bincy saw that her cheeks were hollow, her eyes unnaturally large in her thin face. "You said it wasn't really stealing."

"It isn't, really, Clara," said the boy. He pulled her closer to him, tucking her head underneath his chin. "Hush now. It's all right. Everything will be all right."

Bincy took a step nearer. There was something in the way the boy gently cradled the little girl's tiny body that fascinated her. "Why are you stealing from us?" she asked.

"Because I don't have a choice, Bincy," said the boy. His voice was resigned. "We live on the street. Our parents died years ago – typhoid. It's just me and Clara for it now, and we have to do whatever it takes to stay alive." He tried to smile. "My name is Judd. Judd Winter. This is my little sister, Clara."

"Pleased to meet you," said Bincy automatically, intrigued by the strange meeting. She didn't know if the boy could be dangerous, yet the tenderness with which he was holding his sister made her heart ache for someone to care about her in the same way. She sat down heavily on the floor, feeling drained by their struggle. "Is this the first time you've been in the cellar?" she asked.

"We've been sneaking in here for about a month," said Judd. "I broke a window in the back during the night – it's well hidden behind a big bush. We slip in through there and sleep in the cellar. It's warmer there, and sometimes we can sneak into the kitchen and find some scraps to eat."

He stroked Clara's hair; she seemed to be falling asleep, her head pillowed on his chest. "I know stealing is wrong," he added softly. "But what can I do? Clara's sickly and weak as it is. I have to make sure she gets something to eat." He looked up at her. "It's harder with you down here in the kitchen at this time of night, though. What are you doing here, anyway?"

Bincy couldn't resist talking to him. It had been so long since someone had held a conversation with her that went beyond simply ordering her around.

"When I make mistakes in the day, Ada locks me in a cupboard," she said. "She's the kitchen maid – she's very mean. Then, when she lets me out, I have to keep working until everything is done. I'm only allowed to go to bed if my work is finished. If there's anything that still needs to be done when Ada gets here in the morning, she locks me in the cupboard for even longer."

Pity crossed Judd's face. "You must hardly sleep, then."

"I do a little, in the cupboard, sometimes," said Bincy. She couldn't take her eyes away from his; he was listening so closely. "But I have so many bad dreams. I miss my mama, and Mae, my friend from the orphanage."

"So you're an orphan, too," said Judd.

"Yes. Well, I don't know if Mama is still alive. She left me in a marketplace and I never saw her again. That was four years ago." Bincy took a breath. "Sorry. I'm talking too much. Mae always told me I do that a lot."

"I don't think you're talking too much," said Judd softly, with a gentle smile. His eyes were curious. "I used to think you had a much better life than we do, you know. But I heard you crying the past few nights in here, and it suddenly didn't sound as good anymore."

"At least it's warm in here," said Bincy, trying to smile.

"I suppose," said Judd. He stood up, still holding Clara. "We have to go." Pain crossed his face. "Bincy, I understand if you have to tell the master about us. He'll fix the windowpane and we'll never come back. But please, if you can keep it from him..." His eyes were desperate. "This is the only way we're staying alive since I lost my job at the factory."

Bincy didn't say anything. She just went over to the bread bin and took out the heel of bread that Ada had left her for dinner. It was stale, but at least it was a sizable chunk. She came back over to Judd and held it out to him.

"Here," she said quietly. "I'm sorry it's stale."

Judd's eyes widened. He reached for the bread and paused when his fingertips touched it. His eyes studied hers. "Thank you, Bincy," he said softly.

His pinky finger was brushing against hers. It was the first time someone had touched her, except to slap her, since she'd left the orphanage. She was quiet for a moment, relishing it. "It's a pleasure," she said softly.

"Please. If you can." Judd took the bread. "Don't tell."

Then they were both gone, disappearing into the cellar. Bincy slowly closed the door behind them and leaned against it, breathing a long sigh of relief. Firstly, she wasn't crazy after all – there really had been someone in the cellar.

Secondly, perhaps – just perhaps – she finally had a friend again.

CHAPTER 8

Bincy could still smell something of Judd and Clara as she scrubbed the cellar floor, making sure to get rid of the dirty prints left by their bare feet. She dipped her brush into the bucket again, then scrubbed the suds across the floor, erasing every trace of their existence. Nobody was going to find out about them. They were her secret.

She heard the scullery door creak as Ada came in and took a deep, steadying breath, preparing herself for the tirade that was sure to come.

Footsteps came up to the cellar, and Bincy could almost feel the disapproval radiating from Ada's body as she glared into the small room. After a few moments, she gave a little snort. "Do you think you're going to make me like you better by scrubbing the floor without me asking?"

"No, miss," said Bincy.

"Good, because it's not going to work," said Ada. She moved away, and Bincy heard the bread bin open. Ada's voice dripped with disdain. "You're a big eater for a little scrap, aren't you?"

Bincy's heart leaped. She swallowed, trying to keep the tremor out of her voice. "Yes, miss."

Ada grunted. "I'll remember not to allow you to be so gluttonous again," she snapped.

"Yes, miss," said Bincy, swallowing hard. Ada's words were especially hard to hear considering how empty Bincy's stomach was. Ada moved away from the bread bin, and Bincy was just allowing herself to relax when she heard a sharp intake of breath and steeled herself. That sound always meant trouble.

"What is *this*?" Ada's voice had a trembling calm that was more frightening than her shrieks of rage.

Bincy got up and almost tiptoed over to Ada, and her heart flipped over in fright. Ada was holding a shiny, pure white shard of pottery: a piece of a mug that Bincy had broken in her struggle with Judd last night. She stared up at Ada, mutely horrified. What could she say to explain this now?

"Well?" Ada said. "Answer me."

Bincy swallowed. "A piece of a mug, miss."

"And how did the mug get into pieces?" asked Ada, her eyes dangerous.

Bincy felt herself trembling. She knew she was going to be locked in the cupboard for this, perhaps for a few days in a row. She was just sliding away into despondency when she remembered what that meant—it meant working in the kitchen alone at night, and a chance to see Judd and Clara again. The thought gave her courage. She looked up at Ada, feeling blatant defiance for the first time in her life.

"I broke it," she said.

Ada raised an eyebrow. "You broke it, *what?*"

"I just broke it," said Bincy boldly, omitting the "miss" again. "I broke the mug. It was an accident. I thought I'd swept up the pieces, but I suppose not."

Ada stared at her for a long few moments as if she couldn't quite believe that Bincy was talking back to her. Then she stepped back, raising her chin.

"Well, then, if you want to be so insolent with me, you will have to learn your lesson," she said, her voice cold and clipped. "Finish scrubbing that floor. Then you're going straight to the cupboard – for four hours, this time." Her eyes flashed. "Let's see how insolent you are after that."

Four hours. Bincy knew that meant she would probably get a chance to see Judd that night, and she tried not to smile as she turned away and walked back into the cellar to finish with the floor. She was almost looking forward to her time in the cupboard. And best of all, Ada didn't even know she'd just given Bincy exactly what she wanted.

She would tell Judd and Clara what had happened tonight, and she'd tell them exactly how she felt – that she didn't mind Ada's cruelty if it meant she got to spend time with the two siblings. She'd keep some of her lunch for them, too. Maybe then they would like her.

Maybe then she wouldn't be alone anymore.

※

This time, when Bincy heard the footsteps coming up the cellar, she didn't have to be afraid. Instead, she put down the pan she was cleaning and hurried over to the door to open it a crack.

"It's all right!" she called out softly. "It's only me – Bincy."

Judd gave a sigh of relief and lit the lantern again. In its golden light, he looked exhausted. "Bincy," he said, rubbing his eyes. "You gave us a fright."

"Sorry," said Bincy, backing away. Her heart sank. Had she just ruined their budding friendship already?

"No, no! Don't apologize." Judd smiled. "We're just a little nervous, that's all." He looked around cautiously. "Our windowpane isn't fixed. I... I guess that means that you didn't tell the housekeeper about us."

Bincy smiled at him. "Of course not," she said softly. "You're my friends now."

Judd relaxed visibly. "Thank you," he said, his eyes still gazing into hers. She felt as though a golden spark had leapt between them, and turned away, not knowing what to do with the feeling. Judd grunted as he lifted Clara into his arms. "Do you hear that, darling?" he said. "Bincy says she's going to be our friend now."

Clara nestled her head against Judd's neck and gazed up at Bincy. She had the biggest, darkest, most solemn eyes Bincy had ever seen, and they made her look angelic despite the stringy hair that fell hopelessly around her face.

"I'm glad," she murmured. "We don't have friends."

Bincy touched her arm, smiling at her. Clara reminded her of young Catherine at the orphanage. So frail and fragile. "You do now," she said. "Look, I want to show you two something. Come on into the scullery."

Judd followed her, still cradling Clara on his hip. She led him over to a disused kitchen cupboard. "We only keep a few things in here," she said, opening it up. "I don't think we've used these dishes since I started working here. So I thought it would make the perfect hiding place."

She watched Judd's face as he peered into the gloomy exterior. Bincy had arranged some dishes to make a little nook in the back of the cupboard, hidden at first glance, but when Judd looked closely, she knew he would see two apples and a piece of cheese waiting there for him and Clara. When he spotted the food, his face lit up, and Bincy's heart turned over. He looked at her, his eyes wide with joy. "Oh, Bincy, you didn't have to."

"I wanted to," said Bincy quickly, overjoyed to see his smile. "I wanted to help you. I'm your friend now, right?"

"That's right," said Judd. He reached into the cupboard with his free hand and took out one of the apples. It was round and red, rosy-cheeked as a schoolgirl. "Look at this, Clara," he said.

Clara was gaping at it. "Oh, Judd, can we eat it right now?"

"*You* can eat it right now, love," said Judd, putting Clara down on the floor and holding out the apple.

She shook her head. "No. Not without you."

"Clara." Judd knelt down and pressed the apple into her hand, closing her fingers over it with his own. "There's one for me and one for you. This one is all yours." He kissed her forehead, his eyes closing as if to squeeze down the power of what he felt for his little sister. "Now off you go – go into our warm place in the cellar and eat it up."

"Thank you!" Clara gasped. She pressed the apple to her lips and took a deep, reverent sniff, then looked up at Bincy with an expression that tugged at her heart. "Thank you, Bincy," she said.

Clara scurried off. Judd straightened up again, turning to Bincy with a smile. "I can't tell you what it means to me," he said. "I am never able to give her enough to eat. I wish I could."

"The master and mistress have so much food, Judd," said Bincy. "They throw away enough to feed all three of us every single day, and it's not even spoiled. It's just left over on their plates." She shook her head. "I don't understand it. Why does their little boy deserve to have more food than I do?"

"It's not about deserving, Bincy," said Judd. He put a hand on her arm, and she felt her heartbeat slow as his reassuring touch was steady on her skin. "I don't know why some of us have to go hungry and others have more than enough. I just know that it's not because some of us deserve to have food and others don't. Because if anyone deserves to have everything…" Judd's voice broke, and he stared sadly over at the cellar. "Then my little sister would be the princess of the whole world. She is such a good, grateful, loyal, hopeful little thing, Bincy. I don't know what I'd do without her."

"I don't know what she'd do without you," said Bincy.

Judd shrugged. "I take care of Clara's body," he said. "She takes care of my heart." The warmth of his tone had a powerful affection in it that made Bincy's heart ache. She wished someone would talk about her in that way.

"Anyway." Judd blew out a breath and gave her an awkward smile. "Thank you for getting the food for us. I know it's wrong to steal. I just know it would be even more wrong to let little Clara go hungry."

"I don't mind," said Bincy quickly. "It – it's easier for me than for you. And the master won't even notice. He has so much…" Her voice trailed off.

"I hope so." Judd's hand was still on her arm. He squeezed it gently. "But please don't get caught. We don't all need to be in the same pickle, do we, then?"

Bincy tried to laugh lightly, but the thought of being caught hadn't crossed her mind before. Her stomach lurched as she thought of what Mrs. Davids would do if she caught Bincy stealing. Then she looked at Judd, saw the gratitude in her eyes, and her heart calmed.

"Of course," she said. "I'll be careful."

She didn't quite mean it. What she meant was that she would do anything in the world to keep Judd and Clara as her friends – to never be alone again.

※

The garbage bag was so heavy that Bincy couldn't actually lift it out of the bin in the kitchen. She had to hold the bag closed tightly in one hand – allowing its smelly contents to spill onto the floor was punishable by a few good whacks from Mrs. Davids's cane – and then tip the bin slowly with the other until she could pull the bag out onto the floor. Then, hoping that it wouldn't tear while she was doing so, she had to drag it across the kitchen and out of the servant's entrance into the backyard.

The bag rattled and clanked behind her, tins bumping against each other as Bincy dragged it along the floor. At least it was a little lighter than it had been last week. By smuggling all the leftover food into the nook she'd made for Judd and Clara, Bincy made sure of that. She was aware that her dress was sitting a little more loosely than usual over her midriff, but she didn't really mind. Her dress was sitting awkwardly in many ways in any case – it had suddenly begun to tighten over her chest. A little looseness around her waist didn't bother her.

She dragged the bag out onto the gravel pathway and plodded toward the place near the stables where it would wait to be collected and taken off to wherever garbage went – probably into the river, she mused. At least none of it was edible anymore. She was making sure of that. She had to pause for a moment to let her cramped shoulders relax a little about halfway to the stables, sheltering in the shade of a tree. Dragging this bag never got any easier, but if she stood here for too long, Ada would shout at her. She stretched her arms, trying to work the kinks out of her shoulders, then grabbed the bag again and pulled.

There was a loud snort from beside her. Bincy saw only a blur of gleaming hide and flying hooves. She leapt back, yelping in terror, dropping the bag and taking a few panicky steps away. A huge black horse reared on the path in front of her, its eyes rolling white, mouth gaping as it fought against the bit. At the other end of the reins, to Bincy's absolute horror, she saw the young master. His blonde hair was swept back as he struggled to keep his grip on the frightened horse, and his chiseled jaw was set in an expression of determined concentration. The horse's front feet thudded back to the earth, and it tried to bolt, but from the ground beside him, the young master gave it a firm yank on the reins.

"Stop that!" he ordered, his authoritative voice ringing. "Stand still!"

The horse froze. The big muscles in its shoulder and haunches twitched and its nostrils flared, but otherwise, it didn't move. Bincy held her breath as the young master looked around, frowning. He'd know that she'd spooked the horse, and then there was no telling what he would do. Would he tell Ada? Or would he spare himself the trouble and simply beat her himself?

His eyes rested on hers, and Bincy thought her heart would stop. They were the sharpest shade of green she'd ever seen in her life; the green of new leaves, piercingly set in his proud face, framed by the blond hair that had been shaken from its careful style in his struggle with the horse and now fell down his forehead like misted gold. They stared at her for a second, and she felt him looking at her, the silence stretching between them like a piece of rubber about to snap. She couldn't bear it; nor could she decipher the way he was looking at her, although it made butterflies flutter in her stomach.

"S-sir," she managed at last. "I-I'm so sorry. I didn't mean to spook your horse. I was just taking out the garbage and I didn't see you there, and he must have gotten a fright of the garbage bag or—"

The young master opened his mouth, and Bincy fell immediately silent, steeling herself for the abuse that was coming. Instead, his voice was warm and rough, like honey melting into toast.

"No, don't worry about it," he said, smiling. "That's quite all right." He gave the horse a slap on the neck; it flinched but didn't move. "Shadow can be a real fool sometimes." He shook his head, tossing the hair out of his eyes. "It takes a good master to handle him."

Bincy looked at the enormous horse and felt awed. She couldn't believe the young master had handled him so easily. "You handle him well, sir."

The young master laughed. "Of course, I do."

Bincy stared at him. She was relieved that he wasn't angry, but there was something else in her heart instead; a curiosity that held her to the spot even though she knew she should be scurrying off to do her work. The young master was still looking at her strangely. She cleared her throat self-consciously, and he seemed to snap out of it. A smile spread over his features. It lit up his eyes and left her a little dazzled.

"I don't think I've seen you before," he said. "I'm sure I would have remembered it if I had."

"I'm just a scullery maid, sir," said Bincy, lowering her eyes.

"Oh, I don't care much for that kind of thing, you know," said the young master expansively. He gave a little laugh. "My philosophy tutor would say something ridiculous about us all being human, or something."

Bincy looked up at him, barely able to believe her ears. What was he talking about?

The young master took a step nearer, pulling his horse after him. His smile broadened, making her feel a little dizzy. "I'm Henry, by the way," he said. "Henry Williams. I live here."

"I know," said Bincy, swallowing hard. "I've seen you riding before. From the kitchen."

Henry laughed. "This is the part where you tell me your name, silly."

Bincy looked around nervously. If Mrs. Davids, Ada, or even the mistress saw her, she knew she would be in terrible trouble. She backed away a little, reaching for the garbage bag again.

"I should really be going, sir," she said. "I don't have ideas above my station. It's not proper for me to tell you my name."

"Pshaw!" Henry shook his head. "Proper this, proper that. It's all codswallop. Come on." He grinned at her. "Just tell me your name. It'll be our secret."

Bincy thought of Judd and Clara. They were a secret, too, and she was beginning to think that she liked secrets. She giggled. "All right," she said. "I'm Bincy Hall."

Henry gave a flamboyant bow. "Pleased to meet you, Miss Hall," he said gallantly, giving her a wink that made her stomach turn over. "I'm very happy to have made your acquaintance."

Bincy giggled again, putting on a grand voice. "The pleasure is all mine, Mr. Williams."

"See? I knew there was a little fun in you," said Henry.

"BINCY!" shouted Ada's voice from the kitchens. "What are you doing out there?"

"I'd best be going," said Bincy reluctantly, grabbing the garbage bag.

"I suppose," said Henry languidly. "Just tell her I told you to stand still while I came by with my horse, all right?" He winked again. "Then she won't be able to be angry with you."

"Thank you," Bincy called after him as he jogged off with his horse. She knew she was going to be in trouble anyway as she dragged the garbage bag further along toward the stables, but somehow, she didn't care. She'd just spoken with the young master of the house, and he hadn't been snobbish at all – he was nice and kind, and something about him made her heart beat faster.

Our secret. She smiled, feeling her heart fill with light. Things were finally looking up.

CHAPTER 9

Two Years Later

BINCY TOOK HER TIME IN THE VEGETABLE GARDEN, treading carefully between the rows of vegetables as she pretended to seek out the fattest, most orange carrots in the whole garden for the master and mistress's beef stew dinner. She knelt down, brushing some dirt away from a carrot top. It was ever so slightly green, and she took it as an excuse to move on. As she straightened, Bincy peeped quickly through the hedge toward the lawn. There was nobody there – not yet. She knew that wouldn't last for long. Trying to contain her giggles, she kept moving along the row, selecting a single carrot and pulling it out. Truth be told, all of them were as juicy as this one – but that wasn't why she was lingering in the vegetable patch for so long.

She placed the carrot carefully in the basket on her arm and looked up toward the garden gate. This time, he was there. She felt her entire being light up. It was all she could do not to throw the basket down and run toward him, but she knew she had to contain herself. She looked around casually, pretending to be inspecting more carrots. Only when she was sure that nobody was watching could she scamper over to him, hopping over the rows of vegetables, giggling.

Henry waited at the garden gate, leaning on it with his strong arms. His shoulders had gotten even broader this summer; they strained against his white button-up shirt as he grinned at her, and there was some hair peeping out of his collar.

"Hello, Bincy," he said, his rough voice melting her heart.

"Hello!" Bincy skipped over to him. She had to tilt her head back to look him in the eye. "How are you today?"

"I'm very well, thank you. All the better for seeing you." Henry gave her that smile, the one that made her heart turn cartwheels. "I missed you the last two days." He frowned. "Are you getting tired of seeing me?"

"No!" Bincy reached out and grasped his forearm. "No, no, Henry, please, never say that. Ada was just keeping me so busy in the kitchen, I couldn't have slipped out even if I tried."

Henry gave her a long look. "Are you sure about that?"

"Positive." Bincy clung tightly to his arm. "I promise."

"All right." Henry relented, his smile returning. "Then I believe you. But only because you're the prettiest little flower in this whole garden." He touched her nose with a finger, and Bincy giggled. "You're still too pretty to be a maid, Bincy. One day, I'll make you the lady of a manor house even bigger than this one."

"Oh, I don't want to be a lady," said Bincy.

"Hmm, but what if you could be *my* lady?" said Henry.

Bincy didn't know what to say, but his words made her feel special and loved. She felt her cheeks flushing red hot and took her hand away from his arm. Henry laughed. "Don't be shy," he said. "Instead, tell me that horrible Ada hasn't been locking you up in the cupboard again."

"She always does," said Bincy. She paused. She wanted to tell Henry all about how she really didn't mind being locked in the cupboard; she'd taught herself to sleep quite soundly in there by now. And every evening, after she'd been let out to finish her chores, Judd and Clara came to the house to curl up in the warm cellar for the night—where she could see them. She knew they needed her to help them. But Judd had made her swear that she would never, ever tell anyone, even though she knew good, kind Henry would never do anything to hurt Judd and his sister.

"You're even prettier when you're thinking," said Henry.

Bincy laughed.

Henry reached into his pocket, pulling out a shiny copper coin. He raised an eyebrow. "Penny for your thoughts?"

Two years of keeping both Judd and Henry secret had made Bincy smooth at lying. "I was thinking about how kind you are to me," she said.

Henry laughed. "Here you go," he said, flipping the penny toward her.

Bincy caught it and offered it back, grinning. "And a penny for your thoughts?"

Henry laughed and leaned over the garden gate to kiss her cheek. It was so sudden and unexpected that Bincy almost flinched away. "My dear, my thoughts would rather shock you," he said.

Bincy pressed a hand to her cheek, feeling her blush intensifying. "Wh-what do you mean?" she asked, with a giggle.

Henry just laughed. He leaned over the gate and picked a strand of lavender from the bush growing there, then tucked it behind Bincy's ear.

"There you are," he said. "A sweet and beautiful flower for a sweet and beautiful lady. I picked it, so it was mine. And now I've given it to you."

"Oh, Henry." Bincy took it out from behind her ear and breathed its beautiful fragrance. "I'll cherish it forever and always." She felt dizzy as she gazed up at him. "Nobody has ever given me a flower before."

"You do that," said Henry, laughing. "And I'll cherish you, little Bincy Hall, my hidden treasure." He doffed his hat to her. "The old bat will be looking for me, so I'll be off. See you again whenever I see you again."

He strode off, leaving Bincy in the garden, clutching the lavender, her entire world filled with an excitement that only Henry could give her.

※

BINCY HADN'T BEEN IN THE KITCHEN WHEN ADA HAD called for her. That was why she was still in the kitchen now, even though the hour hand on the clock had long since ticked past the number eleven. Yet even though she knew Ada had hoped to punish her by giving her three whole hours in the cupboard, she couldn't bring herself to be too upset.

She hummed to herself quietly as she scrubbed the big flagstones of the kitchen floor, thinking to the moment's rebellion that had gotten her into this trouble in the first place. She'd told Ada she had been in the lavatory when the kitchen maid had called for her, but in truth, she'd been in the servant's quarters, gently pressing the lavender between the pages of a tattered and dog-eared book. She could still smell its sweetness, still see the sparkle in Henry's eye as he gave it to her, still feel his fingertips on her cheek as he tucked the little flower behind her ear. *My hidden treasure*. His words made her feel special and warm inside, like sunshine glinting on gold. They made her feel like she mattered.

She was so deep in her daydream about Henry that Judd had to knock twice on the cellar door before she realized she hadn't opened it for him and Clara yet today.

"Sorry!" Bincy hissed, scrambling to her feet. She pulled the door open. Like they had every single night for the past two years, Judd and Clara were waiting in the cellar for her. Clara had grown a little, but she still had the big-eyed look of a little girl; Judd's dusting of facial hair had turned into a stenciled shadow on his cheeks, trimmed patchily with the kitchen scissors.

"Good evening," said Judd quietly. He bent down, setting Clara down on the floor. The little girl's arms and legs were no longer as wispy and skeletal as they had been two years ago; in fact, they were almost sturdy now as she put her arms around Bincy's knees and grinned up at her.

"Hello, little one," said Bincy, running a hand through the little girl's curls. "How are you?"

"Hungry," Clara responded, smiling.

Judd knelt down to her level, touching her cheek. "Then you'd better hurry and go and get our food, hadn't you?" he said.

Giggling quietly, Clara hurried over to the shelf where Bincy always hid leftovers and scraps for them. Bincy watched as the little girl scrambled up onto a box to reach the shelf. With an unpleasant jolt, she realized she had forgotten to keep the heel of today's bread for them. She'd been daydreaming so much about Henry that she'd thrown it into the garbage.

"There's not much there today, I'm afraid," she said, grasping for an excuse. "Ada was keeping a sharp eye on me. But I daresay there's something."

"Thank you," said Judd, but his voice was curt and clipped. Bincy felt a pang of worry. Did he know that she'd thrown away the bread?

"I'm sorry," she said, stepping back, hanging her head. "I... I can't always k-keep everything for you. I d-d-do try, but it's..."

"No. Bincy." Judd looked up, and his eyes were a little kinder. He touched her arm. "Thank you for what you've done – truly, I appreciate it."

Bincy frowned. "Then why are you angry with me?" she asked.

"I'm not..." Judd paused. He ran a hand through his long hair, biting his lip as he searched for words. "I'm not angry with you," he said, more gently. "I'm worried for you."

Bincy didn't know what he was talking about. She stared up at him. "Why are you worried for me?" she asked. "It's all right, you know. Ada doesn't really suspect anything. I'm just careful, that's all – and the nights aren't so bad. I sleep in the cupboard when she locks me in there." She smiled. "And I like meeting you in the evenings, too."

"It's not that," said Judd. His eyes were hooded. "I saw that there was someone else you like meeting, too."

His voice was faintly accusatory. Bincy stepped back, feeling the blood rushing to her face. "What do you mean?"

"Don't try that, Bincy," said Judd sharply. "I saw you with the young master. It seems like you two have become quite familiar with each other."

Bincy swallowed, trembling with fear. Was Judd going to give away her secret? She had never told a soul about him and Clara spending nights in the cellar, but it wouldn't be the first time that she'd been betrayed.

"Henry and I are friends," she whispered, unable to lie to his sharp eyes. "Nobody else knows. Please, Judd, don't tell. Ada and Mrs. Davids would be so angry with me."

"I don't want to tell," said Judd sharply. "Who would I tell, anyway? I don't know anyone in this house. But I still don't think it's a very good idea to be friends with the likes of Henry Williams."

Anger flared in Bincy. "What do you mean, *the likes* of him?"

"Oh, come on, Bincy. Can't you see?" snorted Judd. "Why do you think he's become friends with you?"

"Because he's a kind person," said Bincy quickly. "He likes talking to me, and he always says nice things. Not like you." She crossed her arms.

She saw a flicker of hurt in Judd's eyes, but he seemed to brush it away quickly. "I'm telling you, Bincy, that Henry doesn't have good intentions with you. He will use you. Mark my words."

"What?" Bincy's voice rose in indignation. "How dare you say that! Henry is my friend!"

Judd's eyes widened. "Shhh!" he hissed, raising his hands.

Bincy's heart was hammering with anger. "Henry has only ever been kind to me," she spat. "He cares about me. You can't say those terrible things about him!"

"Bincy, be quiet!" snapped Judd.

"How could you say that?" Bincy shouted.

Clara came running up to them, clutching the two oranges that Bincy had scavenged for them. Her eyes were wide. "Someone's coming," she hissed.

Bincy looked up at Judd, feeling the color draining from her face. In her anger, she hadn't even realized she was raising her voice. What had she done?

"Quickly!" she hissed. "You have to get out of here."

Judd didn't need telling twice. He scooped Clara into his arms, running toward the cellar. Bincy could hear footsteps in the hallway now. She half pushed the two of them through the door. Judd spun to face her, and she could see that his eyes were wide and scared in the lantern light as he clutched Clara closely to his chest. Her heart was pounding.

"Go!" she whispered. "Get out of here. I'll stall her."

Judd didn't say anything. He just nodded and hurried toward the back of the cellar. Bincy closed the door and spun around just as Ada walked into the kitchen. The maid's hair was standing on end, mussed with sleep, but there was nothing sleepy about the unadulterated rage pouring out of her expression.

"What are you doing down here?" she shrieked, striding over to Bincy. She was expecting the slap, but it still hurt when it rang across her face. "Don't you understand that I need my rest?"

"S-sorry, miss," stammered Bincy, scrambling for a plausible lie. "I-I saw a rat. A huge big one running out of the cellar." She gulped, praying silently that Ada would believe her. "It was so big, I got such a big fright, and I just panicked and screamed."

Ada's eyes narrowed. "Out of the cellar, you say?" she said, her eyes sliding toward the cellar door.

Bincy's pulse quadrupled. *Please, let Judd and Clara be long gone.* "Y-yes. It ran back in there when I screamed, and I shut it up in there. It had very big teeth," she added quickly.

Ada stepped toward the cellar door. "Let's see about that."

Bincy grabbed her arm. "No!" she gasped. Ada glared at her. "No, please, miss, don't," said Bincy. "It might bite you."

"I think I can handle a rat, unlike you," spat Ada. She shook her arm, throwing Bincy to the floor. Sitting on the cold stones, Bincy could do nothing to stop the kitchen maid as she swung the door open. For a moment, they both stared into the dark cellar, silent. Then, Ada grabbed a gas lamp from the kitchen shelves and held it up inside the smaller room. Bincy felt her heart slowing down. There was nobody there. Judd and Clara had made their escape – and just in time, too.

"Humph." Ada snorted, putting the lamp back on the shelf and closing the door. Her eyes burned with suspicion as she glared down at Bincy. "Seems like there's nothing there – anymore." She gave Bincy another long stare. "Get back to work. And if you wake me again, why, I'll tan your hide for you, you stupid girl."

"Yes, miss." Bincy scrambled to her feet, trembling with relief. "Thank you, miss. I'll do that, miss."

Ada glared at her. "See to it that you do," she snapped.

With that, she flounced out of the kitchen. Bincy leaned against the table, feeling drained. That had been a close call – far too close for comfort – but the tense situation wasn't what left her feeling sick to her stomach.

It was the horrible things Judd had said about Henry, and the look in his eyes as he turned away from her. He had been so angry – angrier than she'd ever seen him in the two years she'd known him. Her stomach knotted with fear. What did it mean for their friendship?

Would they be back?

CHAPTER 10

The next night, they weren't back. Bincy hadn't had to work in the kitchen that night, but she had left them food, and it was untouched the next morning. Trying to quiet the terror that was growing in her stomach like a tumor, Bincy continued to hide the food every night, and every morning, it would still be there. She even checked that the windowpane was still broken, thinking someone might have found and repaired it, but the glass was still missing – and the food was still sitting on the shelf four days later, untouched.

Five days after her fight with Judd, Bincy was desperate. It was the longest she had ever gone without being locked in the cupboard for several hours during the day, and as she chopped vegetables for dinner, she mused that she never would have thought she'd *want* to get locked up. But she did. She glanced up at Ada, who was on the other end of the scullery, packing away some dishes. Bincy looked down at the vegetables on the cutting board, her heart pounding. She knew that she had to do something to get herself into trouble – then when she was let out in the evening to make up her work, she could stay up all night, keeping watch for Judd and Clara.

If only she could tell Henry about them. Henry would know what to do – and he might even help her. She remembered their last meeting the day before. He had been walking his horse back to the stable; she had waited to take out the garbage until she'd heard the hoofbeats on the drive and had met him among the bushes where Ada's glaring eyes couldn't spot them.

"Hello, my little hidden treasure," Henry said when he spotted her. He led the horse over to her and grinned reaching out to brush the stray hair out of her face. He frowned. "What happened to you?"

Bincy raised her hand to the bruise on her cheek, still there – yellow and fading – from Ada's slap a few nights before. "It was Ada," she admitted. "She's very nasty."

Henry's gaze darkened, his blue eyes turbulent as stormy seas. "One day, I'll be the master of this house," he said. "Then you will get the life you deserve." He brushed the bruise lightly with his thumb. "I promise."

Bincy felt as though she would melt right where she stood. She smiled up at him, allowing herself to daydream, even though she knew it could never happen. No matter what, she would still always be a lowly orphan while he was the son of a wealthy lawyer.

Henry put his head to one side, his forehead creasing. "You seem troubled," he said. "What's the matter?"

She almost told him then: that she had had a fight with her only other friend, that she didn't know where he was or if he was all right, that she was worried sick about him. But she had made a promise to Judd, and no matter what, she had to keep her promise.

"Oh, it's just the cold," she had said, trying to smile away her lie. "Nights get so chilly down in the servants' quarters."

Henry sighed. "One day, treasure," he said. "One day you will have a better life." He smiled, taking a step away, although his fingertips lingered on her cheek. "Just you wait."

She had stared after him as he moved away, her heart aching with longing. Maybe, she thought, Henry could make good on his promise in some way. Perhaps, she could be the housekeeper someday. She knew she would be much kinder to her scullery maids than Mrs. Davids was. If only Judd could see that – could know that Henry was friendly and kind, and that Judd had been wrong about him. It was so foolish that they'd argued about something that was so obviously not true.

Looking up at Ada, Bincy clung to the strand of hope that Henry had given her. She took a deep breath, scraping together the flash of courage inspired by that hope, and picked up her chopping board. It was piled high with chopped carrots, and she walked toward the stove where the water was already boiling for them. She made just enough noise so Ada looked up. As soon as she felt the kitchen maid's cold eyes on her, Bincy tripped, slowly and extravagantly. She gave a yelp of fake dismay as the chopping board slid in her fingers, then tilted. The carrots scattered everywhere, bits of them bouncing across the floor, rolling under the tables. She slipped on one piece and fell heavily to her knee, holding her breath.

It had worked. Ada flew up from where she was stacking dishes, her face scarlet with rage. "What are you doing, you stupid girl?" she shrieked. "Look at the mess you've made! Look at this waste! You will scrub them till they shine!"

Bincy didn't have to act like she was scared. Genuine fear wrenched at her gut as she cowered before Ada. Had she gone too far?

"I'm sorry, miss," she whimpered. "It just slipped out of my hands."

Ada snorted. "I'm sure it did, you fool," she snapped.

She reached down and grabbed Bincy by the ear, her cold fingers agonizingly twisting the extremity so that Bincy yelped involuntarily.

"Into the cupboard with you," she hissed, dragging Bincy across the floor. Despite the pain in her ear, Bincy felt a rush of relief. She allowed herself to be thrust into the cupboard and flinched back from the door as it was heavily slammed, sealing her in familiar darkness.

Bincy sank to the floor, leaning against the back of the cupboard and allowing her heart to slow down. Her trick had worked. She was going to be able to wait for Judd and Clara tonight.

***

THE SILENCE IN THE KITCHEN WAS OVERWHELMING. BINCY paced up and down, waiting impatiently. Her work was long since finished; the clock on the wall read a quarter past one, but still there had been no sign of Judd or Clara.

Bincy walked into the cellar, staring at the corner where they usually threw down their blanket and slept a few hours. She could picture them lying there now, the way they had one morning when she'd come down earlier than the others – just in time to warn them to flee. The morning light had come in softly through the broken window, filtered by the leaves of the bush outside, dappling on Clara's smooth face as she lay quietly in a deep sleep. Judd's body was curled around hers, his arm draped protectively around her, the top of her head tucked under his chin as if he was as tight and secure as a tortoise shell around her tiny body. Bincy remembered how her heart had hurt for someone to care for her that way, to protect her that way. Now, the corner was empty, swept clean. Where could they be?

"Where are you, Judd?" Bincy whispered, leaning against the wall. But her only answer was the chirping of the crickets outside. They were gone, and Bincy didn't know why or how she would get them back. The only thing she knew was that she would have to keep looking for them every single night – come what may.

***

Bincy limped down the darkness of the hallway between the servants' quarters and the kitchen. Her left knee was still painful where Ada had hit her with a rolling pin earlier that day after Bincy had burned the onions on purpose, but she felt less pain than confusion. Normally, a transgression like that would get her four hours in the cupboard. But not today.

Her heart filled with puzzlement, Bincy moved as quietly as she could. The fact that she'd been able to sneak out of the servants' quarters without waking Ada was a miracle in itself – normally she could hardly stir without sparking an angry outburst from the older girl. This time, though, Ada hadn't moved, rolled up so tightly in her blankets that Bincy could only see her outline on the bed. It was a small mercy, and Bincy wasn't betting on her luck holding out. She moved on bare feet, padding silently down the hallway toward the kitchen. She had to find Judd and Clara.

She could see the gray outline of the door into the kitchen

when she heard the voices. She paused for a moment, listening closely. Had she imagined it? No – there it was again; someone talking in the kitchen. Or was it *the cellar?* Excitement shot through her veins, and Bincy hurried toward the kitchen, her heart overflowing with joy and relief. Judd and Clara were fine. She was going to come around the corner and see their faces right this moment.

"Judd! Clara!" she called out softly, pulling open the kitchen door and hurrying inside. There was golden light coming from cracks around the cellar door, and she laughed with joy as she ran over to it. "I'm so glad you're safe. I was so—"

Her words died on her lips as she opened the cellar door. There were two figures inside the cellar, one taller and one shorter. But the two faces glaring down at her did not belong to Judd and Clara.

It was Ada and Mrs. Davids.

Bincy felt as though her heart would fail within her. It felt as though it had just melted and was running down her veins into her feet. She stared at them, speechless, her joyous words shriveled and dead on her lips.

"So it *was* you," hissed Ada, her eyes flashing with triumph.

Bincy gulped. She had no idea what to say. She just stared up at the two women with mute appeal, hoping that they could see the terror in her eyes, hoping it would convince them to be gentle.

It didn't. With disconcerting suddenness for a woman of her bulk, Mrs. Davids lurched forward. Bincy tried to duck, but she was too slow. A cruel hand closed like a vice over her arm, making her yelp in pain as Mrs. Davids pinned her up against the cellar wall.

"Explain yourself," she spat, leaning so close to Bincy's face that droplets of moisture spattered on her cheek.

Bincy's heart was suddenly going again now, and it was racing, galloping, fleeing away into the distance. She gasped for air. "Mrs. Davids—" she began.

"I want the truth, you little thief!" thundered Mrs. Davids, pinning her harder against the wall. Bincy could feel her skin bruising under the housekeeper's vicious grip. "Was it you that broke the window and let those two urchins in here?"

Bincy's heart sank. So, they had found them. "Where are Judd and Clara?" she gasped.

Mrs. Davids' eyes narrowed. She leaned in even closer; Bincy cowered away from her.

"Know their names, do you?" she purred, her voice low as a dagger to the belly. "What else do you know about them, hmm? Was it you who let them in?"

Bincy was shaking uncontrollably. "Where are they?" she whimpered, her worry for them overriding her terror. "What did you do with them?"

"Oh, *we* did nothing with them," said Ada. "The police, on the other hand..." She gave a laugh; a cruel and twisted thing.

"Where have they been taken?" screamed Bincy. A terrible image flashed across her mind: Judd and Clara taken to the gallows. She could almost picture Judd's sad eyes staring at her as they put the noose around his neck, see his feet kicking as the life was choked out of him...

"Oh, you needn't worry about your little friends," said Ada. Her eyes were sadistic. "They'll be quite safe now, somewhere that they'll have food to eat and a place to call home." She laughed again. "The workhouse."

The workhouse. It was better than the gallows, but only marginally. Bincy closed her eyes as an agony that was almost physical pierced her to the very soul. She'd heard all kinds of stories about the workhouse – about the punishments, the food, the sleepless nights – but worst of all, she knew that Judd and Clara would be separated. She could hear Clara's screams as she was ripped out of Judd's arms. They sounded like the screams of a little girl, torn away from her mother, abandoned on streets that didn't want her...

"Answer me!" Mrs. Davids' roar yanked Bincy out of her reverie. "Was it you?"

"Of course, it was her," scoffed Ada, shaking her head. "Who else would it be, ma'am? Look at her eyes. You can see the guilt in them. She's been stealing from our house. She's been fraternizing with thieves all this time." Ada's eyes narrowed. "She should be hanged."

Bincy felt numb. Nothing could feel worse than knowing what was about to happen to Judd and Clara because of her. The housekeeper regarded her disdainfully for a few minutes.

"Handing her over to the police is just too much trouble," she said. "I think I have a punishment of my own that will be just as effective." Her eyes slid sideways to the walking stick that leaned against the shelves of the cellar, and Bincy knew what was coming.

She wept as Mrs. Davids was beating her, the stick's blows thundering down on her back, crashing across her ribs with a force that knocked the breath from her. She cried relentlessly, her sobs renewed with each blow, and when it was done and they left her curled up on the cold kitchen floor, she cried all the more. Her tears streaked and smeared across the floor alongside her blood, but it wasn't for her blood that she was weeping. It was for her friends.

The friends she had lost.

PART III

CHAPTER 11

Judd was sitting at the head of the table. The light from the crystal chandelier above sparkled brightly in his gray eyes, turning their sorrowful shade into something that scattered and glittered like jewels. He was smiling, a half-grin that lit up the entire room with its contentment, as he carved the goose. It was golden, cooked to a turn; when he plunged his knife into it, a plume of fragrant steam rose into the air. The aroma was mouthwatering, and Bincy leaned closer, taking a deep sniff.

"Oh, Bincy, you did such a good job!" exclaimed little Clara, sitting across from Bincy. She was wearing a soft blue gown that draped gently along her tiny body, and her cheeks were plump and rosy, her eyes alive with joy. "This goose is perfect. It's going to be delicious."

"I concur," spoke another voice. Bincy looked to her right, where Henry was sitting. He tossed his head, shaking back a shock of his golden hair. His dazzling smile seemed to fill Bincy's soul with rainbows and dancing, color and music. "It looks magnificent, my love." He put his arm around her, and Bincy nestled against him, feeling joy and contentment blossom in her heart like the unfurling of a red rose.

"A toast is fitting, I think," said Judd. He picked up his glass; it glittered in the light of the chandelier.

"A toast, a toast!" Clara jumped to her feet, holding up a cup of milk.

Bincy laughed. What a splendid idea! She lifted her glass, feeling Henry echo the movement beside her.

Judd gazed at them all solemnly for a moment. His expression was serious, but Bincy could see in his eyes that his soul was reverberating with joy.

"To friendship," he said at last, his voice filled with authority.

"To friendship!" Clara and Henry chorused, Clara's high flute mingling perfectly with Henry's deep bass.

"To friendship," said Bincy, laughing. "To friendship forever!"

They all laughed together, and the sound of their laughter filled Bincy's entire world. It was musical and happy, content and loud, shrill, noisy, constant, clanging—

Bincy sat up with a gasp, the sound of the morning bell deafening in her ears as she stared wildly around the servant's quarters. There was no banqueting table here, no crystal chandelier, and certainly no friends. Just her narrow bunk; Ada's beside her, which was like sleeping in the same room with some deadly serpent; and another cold, gray, wintry day ahead.

Bincy's eyes filled with tears. Her dream had felt so real. She could still smell that goose, still feel Henry's arm around her, still see the color in Clara's face. But it hadn't been real, of course. She hadn't seen Judd or Clara in the two years since the housekeeper and Ada had discovered them in the cellar, and she knew they weren't happy and content the way they had been in her dream – if they were even alive at all. Bincy's heart broke. It felt like she was losing them all over again.

She heard Ada's shoe coming and ducked. It bounced off the wall beside her and landed in her lap. Angry at having missed Bincy's head with her throw, Ada scowled at her.

"Get up!" she ordered. "What are you lying around in here for? You had better have that fire going before I get into the cold kitchen, or you'll feel more than just my shoe, you stupid girl."

"Yes, miss. Sorry, miss," said Bincy, dragging herself out of bed. She straightened up and paused for a moment, staring at Ada. It had been five years since she had come to Williams Manor, and she realized, with a start, that she was taller than

Ada was now. And likely older than the kitchen maid had been then.

"What are you looking at?" Ada spat. "Get out of here!"

Bincy hurried off, resigning herself to the fact that she was doomed to be a hated scullery maid forever. And it truly seemed as though everyone in the manor house hated her. They all took Ada's side on everything, and as far as the other servants were concerned, Bincy was as dishonest as she was lazy. She felt her isolation all around her, like a frozen wasteland extending in all directions. Mama had abandoned her. Mae had betrayed her. Even Judd, who had been her closest friend, had turned against her.

There was only one person in all the wide world who cared for her, and it was Henry. Bincy closed her eyes for a moment as she knelt by the hearth, allowing a pang of both happiness and longing to rush through her. It had been months since he'd bid her farewell, but she could still feel the pressure of his hands on hers, still see the softness in his face as he gazed into her eyes.

"Don't go," she had begged him, clinging to his hands. "Please. I need you here."

"Oh, treasure." Henry sighed, touching her cheek, pushing his hand between her hair and her neck so that goosebumps rose on her skin. "I don't want to go, but I have no choice. I have to get an education if I'm going to keep this manor house and give you the life that you truly deserve one day." He leaned closer and kissed her forehead. The scent of his cologne surrounded her like embracing arms.

"I'll be back," he whispered. "As soon as the Christmas holidays come, I'll be back here with you. I'll think of you every day, Bincy. You'll never leave my thoughts, and before you know it, I'll be back from university and you'll be in my arms again."

Then he had gone, leaving Bincy alone by the garden gate, feeling as though her very breath had left her lungs to go with him. She lit the fire with trembling hands. Somehow the world was so much colder, so much darker without Henry.

But it was winter, at least; that much she knew by the glow of starlight on the snow outside, the pang of the cold in her hands and feet. That meant Christmas couldn't be far away. And Henry – her beautiful, wonderful, faithful Henry – would be back soon.

"Only a little while," she murmured to herself in encouragement as the flames began to lick around the firewood that had been stacked in the hearth. "Not much longer, and he'll be back."

That knowledge was the only thing getting her from one day to the next.

BINCY WASN'T AT ALL SURPRISED THAT THE OTHER MAIDS

had left her alone in the scullery, washing dishes, on this rare day of sunshine. Outside, she knew the maids were clearing the brambles, taking out the garbage, doing anything that would bring them out to where the sun was glittering on the freshly fallen snow, slowly melting it into gray slush. Tomorrow, it would be cold and icy out there again, unpleasant with mud and slush, and she knew she'd be sent to do the work outside then. But today, she was stuck in the frigid kitchen, continually adding hot water to the sink in the hopes that her numb fingers wouldn't be completely frozen as she washed dishes.

At least she knew Christmas had to be coming soon. The master had come home with a beautiful pine tree the other day, and on the rare occasions that she walked past the main hall, she'd seen it set up in a corner and draped in baubles and tinsel and candles. Christmas itself was nothing to her. Nobody ever gave her gifts, and Ada usually locked her in the closet so she couldn't attend the church service. But Christmas meant Henry, and Henry was the only warm place her heart knew to run to when she felt like the whole world was like this kitchen – cold, gray, and lonely.

The door to the main house opened, letting a rush of warm air into the scullery. Bincy didn't look up, redoubling the speed that she was washing the dishes. Mrs. Davids coming into the scullery was never a good thing. She kept her head down as she scrubbed at the fine China in her hands, gross bits of old food swirling through the dirty water and bumping queasily against her bare skin.

She heard footsteps moving across the floor, and a cold sweat broke out under her shabby dress. Why was Mrs. Davids walking so slowly? What had she found to criticize about what Bincy was doing? She swallowed hard, trying to contain her panic, but her heart fluttered madly against her ribs like a sparrow in the cruel grip of a schoolboy.

Mrs. Davids was coming closer. Bincy's hands were clumsy with fear now. A plate slipped through her fingers and plunged into the water with a splash, sending droplets of dirty water splattering over her dress. She heard it bump against the bottom of the sink and her heart swooped. Whether it was chipped or not, Mrs. Davids would be furious. She could hear her breathing now, right behind her, and feel the air move as the woman raised a hand to strike her -

But when the hand descended on her shoulder, it was big and warm, not Mrs. Davids' angry claw.

Bincy whirled around, her fluttering heart stilled, and looked up into a pair of eyes that were as blue and bright as the winter sky. She gave a cry of shock and joy. "Henry!"

"Hello, my little treasure," said Henry, grinning.

Bincy felt as though the whole world had turned upside down in the most glorious way. She threw herself at him, throwing her arms recklessly around his torso. He was so warm, so solid. She buried her face in his chest as he returned her embrace, his laughter vibrating through his body. Taking a deep breath, she was a little surprised to find that he smelled different somehow — there was a fruitiness to his aroma, a strange tang she didn't recognize. But it didn't matter. He was still Henry, her wonderful, kind and friendly Henry, and when he stepped back, his eyes were shining.

"I missed you so much," Bincy gushed. She saw that his hair was combed differently, the top leaning over to one side in an elegant curve, instead of slicked back the way it had been before he'd gone. "I've been thinking about you every single day."

"And I've been doing the same," said Henry, beaming. He touched her cheek; she leaned into his warm hands. "My carriage stopped here last night, so I've been here since then. I've been trying to shake Mother off so that I could come and see you."

Bincy paused, a little startled by his boldness coming into the kitchen. She felt flattered. "Thank you for coming down here to see me. You — you've never done that before."

"Oh, I've always been too nervous." Henry laughed. "But university made a man out of me. Now nothing is going to stop me, my precious." He caressed her cheek, leaning a little closer. "You're my beautiful little treasure. All mine, and as stunning as you were when I left."

His words made Bincy feel warm inside, but he was suddenly

very close, and coming ever closer. She froze, confused, her heart pounding. His breath was warm on her cheek, and then his lips were touching hers, and a jolt of panic ran through her. She stepped back quickly, pressed against the sink.

"H-Henry," she stammered.

Henry pulled back. Regret lanced through Bincy when she saw the hurt in his eyes. "I'm sorry," he said, his voice filled with pain. "I-I thought you liked me... in that way."

"I do!" Bincy reached out, grasping his shirt to stop him from walking away. "I do, Henry."

Henry stared down at her. "So, what's the matter? Didn't you miss me?"

"I missed you every day. Please, don't say such things. You know I care for you," said Bincy.

"So? Why are you pulling away?" Henry demanded. "Don't you love me?"

"Of course, I love you." Bincy couldn't explain why she was suddenly so frightened, or why his hands on her waist felt so invasive instead of tender, why his grip around her hips made her tremble for fear instead of pleasure. She tried to push the feelings away. Why was she being such a fool?

Henry leaned against her, the length of his body against hers, his eyes burning. "Then let me love you," he murmured, and his lips were on hers, his hands grasping her waist, pulling her closer.

Bincy felt her heart hammering, but she couldn't tell whether she was feeling excitement or fear. His kiss was demanding, promising more, and she didn't know how to respond, but she knew she couldn't pull away no matter how much she wanted to. So, arms still around his torso, she just allowed him to kiss her as her feelings clashed and thundered inside her.

He was breathless when he pulled back at last, his eyes sparkling. "I missed you, my treasure."

Bincy wanted to wipe her mouth, but she just smiled at him instead. "I missed you, too."

There were footsteps in the hallway from outside, and it was with a shock that Bincy realized she almost felt relieved to hear Ada coming. Henry stepped back, looking reluctant.

"I'll be back, my little beauty," he said, and hurried back into the house.

Bincy realized that there were tears in her eyes when she turned back to the sink, and she couldn't think why. Hadn't Henry just shown her how much he loved her? How much he'd missed her?

Yet she couldn't shake one idea from her mind: the thought that somehow, Henry was different. And the worry that he might not be her kind and friendly Henry anymore.

CHAPTER 12

It was just as Bincy had known it would be: a cold, gray, slushy day, with sleet falling gently through the sky, only to turn into icy droplets that ran down the leaves of the trees and the roof of the house, splashing onto the frozen ground, leaving it slick and precarious. It was no surprise when Mrs. Davids told her curtly to take the garbage out.

Bincy lugged the heavy bag reluctantly out of the house, slipping and struggling on the frozen mud. Ada had left the chicken out for too long – and Bincy had, of course, been blamed for it – and the stench of the rotten meat hung in the cold air as she staggered along the long path. She hoped nothing was going to fall out of the bag. She hated having to grab scraps of slimy, smelly garbage to put them back into the bag.

The path was slippery under her feet, and she felt like she could fall over at any moment. For the past few days, her life had felt like that, too – her relationship with Henry as uncertain as her footing. She had no idea what to think of what had happened the first day he'd been home, so much so, that she'd been avoiding him. She loved him so much, and she had missed him dearly. Yet there was something about him that hadn't been there when he'd left. Something hungry. It frightened her a little, and she didn't know what to do.

Right now, she had to pay attention to where she was putting her feet. A naked toe poked out of a hole in her left shoe as she struggled on, trying to avoid the mud, holding out an arm to hold her balance on the ice. It was a relief to move into the trees and bushes near the stables, where she could at least grab onto a branch if it felt like she might fall.

The next moment, he was beside her, firm hands grasping her waist and lifting her into the air. Bincy gave a little squeal of panic and excitement, dropping the garbage bag and grabbing for Henry's shoulders as he spun her, holding her almost above his head. She was dizzy when he finally stopped and put her down, laughing.

"Hello, my treasure," he said, his voice deep and beautiful. "I've missed you the last few days."

"Henry!" Bincy giggled, leaning giddily against the tree behind her. For the step back she took, he took two steps forward, staying close to her. "I didn't see you there."

"Your face is so pretty when you're concentrating," said Henry. He reached for a corkscrew curl of hair that hung by her face and wound it around his finger; where his fingertip brushed accidentally against her cheek, it made Bincy's heart beat wildly.

"I've been following you for a while now."

Bincy wasn't sure what to make of that statement. "Why?" she asked, laughing lightly. "Why only surprise me now, then? I've been missing you, too."

His eyes darkened. It wasn't rage, exactly, that crossed his face, but it was an intensity – a hunter's look. He moved closer to her, and she felt suddenly trapped against the tree. "Because here's where we have a little privacy," he murmured.

Then he was kissing her again. Bincy was ready for it this time, still a little dizzy from the spinning, still a little breathless with the look in his eyes, and she struggled to breathe. His kiss was aggressive, relentless; it pressed her back, making her feel trapped. She felt his hands on her waist, clutching, possessive. The hands pressed against his chest didn't seem to communicate the word that was spinning in her mind: *Stop*. She knew how improper it was. The master's son kissing the scullery maid – it was scandalous. But he was kissing her, passionately, and now his hands were creeping up her waist, reaching her ribs, his fingers crawling ever higher, and she couldn't breathe, and her head was spinning, and she wanted to cry out—

"Look at this!" Ada's angry voice rang through the air. "Look at the garbage lying here! Where is that foolish girl?"

Henry pulled back. Bincy took a gasp of the wonderful, pure, cold air. Henry's eyes grew angry, but he turned back to her and gave her a peck on the forehead.

"We'd better be off," he murmured. "But don't you worry, my treasure." He touched her chin. "I'll be back for you."

He disappeared, and Bincy hurried back to the path, pulling her bonnet strings tight again. Ada was staring in the path, her face filled with disgust as she stared at the garbage bag lying there. "You!" she barked. "Where on earth were you?"

"S-sorry, Ada," said Bincy, scrambling to pick up the bag. A chunk of the rotten chicken had fallen out, and goosebumps burst across her body as she scooped it back inside with her bare hands.

"Answer me, you fool," snapped Ada.

"I-I-I…" Bincy had no idea what to say. She stared up at Ada, completely tongue-tied.

A twig snapped. Bincy froze, hearing a hurried footstep behind her. She didn't turn around. She didn't need to. Ada's expression told her everything that she needed to know: that she'd seen Henry.

Ada knew.

BINCY HAD KNOWN ALL AFTERNOON THAT ADA HAD TOLD the housekeeper. Usually, nobody ever spoke to Bincy, but now, they directly avoided her. The other scullery maid stared at her. The parlor maid ducked down a random doorway when she saw Bincy coming down the hall. Bincy felt like she had a disease, something horrible and infectious, something that the others were terrified of catching. And all afternoon, every time Mrs. Davids passed her, she gave her the kind of look that made Bincy feel like something squishy that Mrs. Davids had just stepped in.

Yet nobody said anything. Bincy plucked the goose, boiled the broth, cut the vegetables, washed the dishes. She cleaned the stove, swept the floor, did it all as silence echoed around her, as the cold stares crucified her. She didn't know what to do with herself. She felt as though her anchor point was loose, as if the only pillar left that held up her world – the cornerstone of her life – was suddenly shaky.

It was almost a relief that evening when all the others had left the kitchen and Bincy found herself alone with Mrs. Davids and Ada. She turned around slowly, wiping her greasy hands on a dishcloth. When she looked up at Mrs. Davids, her eyes weren't angry. They were cold – cold and immovable, like frosted stone.

Mrs. Davids didn't waste time on formalities. She just walked across the room, drew back her arm and delivered a back-handed slap across Bincy's face so fast that she didn't even have time to brace herself. Bincy reeled back, stars popping across her eyes as she lost her footing and fell to one knee, automatically raising a hand to her face. Something warm touched her skin, and she stared down uncomprehendingly as blood slithered between her fingers. Her lip was throbbing.

"How could you," hissed Mrs. Davids, her voice low, cold and dangerous. "How could you have done this? Does this look like a brothel to you, girl?"

Bincy stared up at her. "I didn't—" she began.

Mrs. Davids slapped her again. Bincy felt the slit in her lip widen and clapped her hand over her mouth, catching the pooling blood. Tears of pain filled her eyes, and her lip wasn't what was hurting her. It was no use. Trying to explain to Mrs. Davids that she'd done nothing wrong would be useless. She just crouched on the floor, feeling the blood trickle down her chin, trembling mutely as Mrs. Davids stood over her. The woman's breathing was harsh with rage.

"You will be thrown on the streets, that much is for sure," she snarled. "Perhaps then you will find your way to one of the houses of ill repute where you belong. But first, you will pay for your appalling behavior." She held out a hand, and Ada, wearing a wide grin on her face, placed a broomstick in her hand.

Bincy had felt the broomstick before. She cowered, bracing herself for it, feeling tears and blood mingle on her face.

Fighting would be useless. Everything was useless. Henry was just like the rest – just like Judd and Mae and Mama: ready to betray her at any moment. She heard the broomstick whistle through the air as Mrs. Davids raised it and cringed in readiness for the first blow...

"STOP!"

Henry's voice thundered through the kitchen, loud and ringing with authority. Bincy looked up, gasping with surprise. He stood in the doorway, lit from behind so that his golden hair seemed to be a halo of fire around his head, but his eyes burned brighter. He strode over to Mrs. Davids and seized the broomstick from her. Planting a hand on her shoulder, he shoved her back so that she staggered and fell onto her rear.

Henry was shaking with anger. "You won't lay a finger on that girl," he growled. "Not for one moment."

Bincy scrambled to her feet. Henry had the broomstick raised, and for a frightening moment, she thought he was going to use it. Instead, he snapped it over his knee, the crackle of wood making Ada's eyes widen with fear. He flung the broomstick down on Mrs. Davids' face, making her gasp in pain and fright.

"You don't touch that girl," he growled, glaring down at Mrs. Davids. "I am your master. You're just here to do whatever I tell you, and I'm telling you now to leave the scullery maid alone. If you raise a hand to her – and if you tell my parents – I will know." His eyes narrowed. "You are not to breathe a word of this to anyone. No one in the world. Do you understand?"

Mrs. Davids opened her mouth, a flash of anger coming back into her eyes. Moving so fast he almost blurred, Henry grabbed her by her cap, pinning her back down to the ground. "Do you understand?" he spat in her face.

Mrs. Davids's eyes were wide with something Bincy had never seen in them before: open fear. She nodded mutely, not looking away from Henry even for a moment.

"Good," snapped Henry. He let her go, and she sank to the floor, trembling visibly. He strode over to Bincy, putting a hand on her cheek. His eyes dwelt on her split lip for a moment, disappointment visible in his face. "Don't you worry, treasure," he said, kissing her forehead. "Soon those pretty lips will be kissable again."

"Oh, Henry," Bincy gasped, clutching his hands. "Oh, thank you."

Henry's eyes flashed with something dangerous. "Thank me later," he smiled, and then he was gone. Bincy didn't look down at Mrs. Davids or Ada. Instead, she just ran back to her room in the servants' quarters, her heart hammering with joy as she staunched the bleeding from her lip. Henry had saved her. His passion was nothing but a symptom of his love, Bincy was convinced – he had protected her from her worst enemies, and he cared about her enough to do anything for her.

She tried not to think of the fear in Mrs. Davids's eyes, or about the fact that Henry didn't want his parents to find out about her. She just thought of his strong arms and his bright blue eyes, and she was no longer free-falling through space. Her fingers had found something familiar, something solid. And she was going to cling onto it with everything she had.

CHAPTER 13

During her precious and scant free time, Bincy had been waiting for nearly an hour in the secret corner of the garden, the hidden spot by the gate that was shielded by the privet hedge and a few elm trees from the prying eyes inside the house and kitchen. Her heart was fluttering with excitement as she peered between the branches of the elm at the main door of the house. Any moment now, Henry, her savior, would be coming out of that door to see her – and she couldn't wait.

The memory of what he'd done for her last night was something so precious that she almost didn't want to think about it too much, the same way that she didn't take her piece of lavender out of the pages of her book too often – as if it would crumble to dust if she handled it too regularly. But like the lavender, she knew it was there, all the time, a precious thing that was all hers. Another gift from her beloved Henry.

At last, as the rich evening sun was touching the frozen landscape with a kiss of gold, she saw him. The light made his hair blaze like spun sunshine as he hurried across the lawn toward her. His eyes were intense, but she tried not to look at them. Instead, she focused on the wide smile that he wore as he rushed up to her.

"Henry!" Bincy couldn't bring herself to stand still. She pushed through the garden gate and ran to him. Henry laughed, opening his arms wide, and Bincy ran into them without hesitation. He spun her so that her skirts swirled around her legs, laughing. She felt that familiar dizziness as he put her down and gazed into her eyes.

"Thank you so much," Bincy gasped, clinging to him. "Thank you."

"Those women didn't do anything to you, did they?"

"Not a thing," said Bincy. "It worked. You told them to leave me alone – and they did." She laughed in disbelief and joy. "You saved me, Henry. Thank you so much."

"Of course, I would have to save you." Henry grinned, leaning closer to her. He rested his forehead on hers, and she felt her heart pounding, this time with excitement. "You're my hidden treasure."

Bincy draped her arms around his neck, giggling. "All yours," she told him, a little breathless with the closeness of him, with the feel of his hands on her back.

His touch changed suddenly, becoming possessive. He pulled her against him more quickly than she wanted. "And now you owe me," he whispered.

Bincy swallowed. That change in him – it was there again, something dark and violent as he stared into her eyes.

"What do I owe you?" she said, trying to sound playful.

"Oh, I think you know," said Henry.

She still wasn't ready for it when he started to kiss her, and this time he kissed her like he wanted to become a part of her. She took a step back and he pressed her up against the garden fence, his lips insistent, unforgiving as they explored hers. She tried to relax. She tried to kiss him back, to enjoy the feel of his hands crawling over her, but they moved higher and higher on her dress, sneaking to a place where they didn't feel right. Her excitement turned to panic. She braced her hands against his shoulders and pushed him back, staggering away, panting.

"What is it?" Henry asked. He scooped her effortlessly back into his arms, ignoring her squirming. "What's the matter?"

"Henry, please." Bincy was shaking. "Just – slow down."

"Why?" Henry's eyes were dangerous. He touched her lip, pulling her against himself. "Don't you want me, treasure?"

She didn't. Not like this – not the way he was now. But she couldn't bring herself to say it to him. She didn't have much time, in any case; he only stared at her for a moment before kissing her again, and this time his hands were creeping up her arms, to the neck of her dress, to the button at her throat. She felt the gentle release of the cloth around her neck as the button was undone, his fingers on her skin—

"Henry!" shouted a voice. With a tide of relief, Bincy recognized the mistress.

Henry gave an animal growl of frustration. "What does she want?" he muttered.

"Henry, dear, come in!" the mistress called. "Dinner is about to be served!"

Henry turned back to Bincy and gave her another long, yearning glance. She could feel his eyes on her, as unwelcome as his touch.

"Don't you worry, treasure," he said, grinning at her. He kissed her one more time. "I'll be back for you."

The inflection in his words was loud and evident, and so terrifying that as soon as Henry had turned his back, Bincy sank to the ground. She ignored the snow that seeped into her dress, covering her face with her hands as uncontrollable sobs gripped each breath, shaking her mercilessly, threatening to choke her.

What was she doing? What was Henry doing?

And worst of all, if Henry had his way, then what would she become?

Tears poured down Bincy's cheeks as she stuffed her things into a ragged cloth bag. The bag was small, but there wasn't much to take: her single extra dress; a cake of soap as small and hard as a shilling; three copper pennies; an extra bonnet with a hole in it; and, last of all, her book. She picked it up quickly, her hands clumsy with grief and fear, and the pages fell open. Soft as a whisper, the lavender tumbled out and landed lightly on the floor. A few of the dried petals broke off and crumbled beside it.

Bincy sank to the floor, staring down at the lavender as she sobbed. Part of her wanted to leave it lying there. Hadn't Henry wanted to use her, just like everyone else? She straightened up, stuffing the book into her bag, and turned away. Yet turning her back on that flower – turning her back on Henry – made her feel like she was ripping something away. Like she was tearing off a part of herself. With a little sob, she turned back and scooped the lavender into her hands. She held it close, and it still smelled sweet, with the innocent memories of her time with Henry before he went to university and everything changed.

She would give anything to go back to that time. But she couldn't go back. Not now, and not ever. Things had changed – *Henry* had changed, and she couldn't bear the thought of what he might do to her if she stayed.

She lifted the bag onto her shoulder, tightened the strings of her bonnet and walked purposefully through the kitchen. For the first time, she strode out smartly, her shoes clopping on the floor. Ada didn't have any power over her now; nobody did. She wasn't being thrown out. With a shock, Bincy realized that for the first time in her life, she was throwing herself out. She was going where she wanted to go, not where she was taken.

It was that thought alone that gave her the courage to walk through the kitchen. Every eye – every maid and waiter and cook and cleaner – was watching her. She threw back her shoulders and held up her head and strode toward the door, swallowing down her tears. Nobody made a single move to stop her. And before Bincy knew it, her feet had carried her all the way to the street and out into the sunshine with the light sparkling off every snowdrift and every icicle in the cold street. The wind was icy, but there was something delicious in it, in knowing that her own feet had borne her out to this moment.

Bincy raised her head, trembling with fear, not knowing what the night would bring or how the next day would come. But for right this moment, the cold breeze was enough. She drank it in. It tasted of something entirely unfamiliar.

It was freedom. And it was intoxicating.

Bincy had no idea even which way to wander. The

last time she'd been on the streets of London had been five years ago, when Mrs. Price had first brought her here. Now, it seemed like a labyrinth of streets, each one more fascinating than the next.

In a single day, Bincy had seen and heard more than she had in the rest of her life. There were carriages and children running and a marketplace surrounded by stalls that were filled with more color than she'd ever seen before. There were strangers and cheerful newspaper vendors and dogs. One of the dogs ran up to her and allowed her to touch its face, and she couldn't believe how much joy there seemed to be in its eyes. How was there that much joy in all the world?

And the music. There was a gray-haired woman standing on a street corner, her clothes just as shabby as Bincy's, her hat on the ground at her feet, a few coins glinting inside. She had one eye missing and the side of her face was a mess of scars. She was playing an old, worn violin, as decrepit as she was, but the sound. The sound was as bright as the light in her eye, and it seemed to call out to Bincy's very soul. She spent a long time just standing there and staring at the woman, listening to the music. Of course, she had heard snatches of it before, up in the manor house. But up close, it was like nothing she'd ever heard before. It was more than just a melody – it was color made into sound.

She tried to stay away from anywhere that seemed too smelly or reminded her of the slum where she'd been born, but she never stood still for too long, except to listen to the woman with the violin. Every step was new and exciting and free, but as the day began to wear to a close, something new started to grip her: fear. The old, familiar panic of enclosing walls was surrounding her again, even though the open streets stretched in every direction all around her. As her tired legs slowed down, her thoughts finally caught up to her.

Where was she going to sleep tonight? What was she going to have for dinner? Suddenly, those three pennies in her pocket seemed useless.

Bincy didn't know what else to do, so she walked up to the first manor house that she saw. A powerful bulldog barked at her from behind a palisade fence as she followed the twisting little path around to the servants' entrance. That, at least, was easy to recognize; Bincy guessed servants everywhere were given a tiny, narrow door that had cobwebs in the corners and seemed to be permanently cloaked in shadow.

It took her several seconds to pull together the courage to knock. When the door opened, the woman who answered it was rake-thin and had a great, prominent nose, like some scrawny owl glaring down at her from a lamp-post. Yet the eyes themselves, when Bincy could bring herself to look into them, were kindly. They gave her the scrap of courage she needed to speak.

"Good evening, m-m-ma'am," she managed.

"Good evening." To Bincy's surprise, the woman's tone was pleasant. "How can I help you?"

"I-I don't need help," Bincy hurried to say. "I'm just looking for a job. I'd like to speak to the housekeeper, if you please."

"I am the housekeeper," said the woman gently. "What kind of work are you looking for?"

"I'd like to work as a scullery maid, ma'am." Bincy gulped. "I've been a scullery maid for five years. I'm a hard worker, and I don't like to get into trouble." *Even though I'm always in trouble*, she added to herself.

"That sounds interesting," said the woman. "And who are your references?"

References? Bincy felt like she'd just been punched in the gut. Where was she supposed to find references? Mrs. Davids would rather eat her own feet than vouch for her; in fact, if she told this housekeeper that she'd worked at the Williams manor, Mrs. Davids would tell her exactly what she thought of her, and her bad reputation would spread like a cancer. That was if it wasn't spreading already. Suddenly Bincy didn't feel free anymore. She just felt free-falling again, and there was nothing around her to grab onto. Her anchor point wasn't just wobbly anymore – it was gone.

The housekeeper saw the panic in her eyes. Her face filled with a kind of resigned pity. Bincy saw her studying her scuffed shoes, worn dress, and the tiny bag in her hand. "You're not going to get anywhere without references, dear," she said sadly. "Even if I wanted to hire you, I can't. Mistress won't allow anyone to be employed without references. That's just how the world works, I'm afraid."

Bincy swallowed. "What do you think I should do?" she asked. She knew that this housekeeper was a stranger, but she had to ask someone, and hers was the only kind face she'd seen in a very long time.

The housekeeper looked away. "There's not much you can do," she murmured. "There's a workhouse a few blocks from here, though."

"A workhouse?" Bincy's heart flipped over. She thought of how fearfully the girls in the orphanage, as well as Judd and Clara, had always spoken of that place. With a pang of sadness, she realized that at least she didn't have anyone to be separated from. But what about the punishments they'd spoken of? The canings? She closed her eyes briefly, remembering her time in the refractory ward back at the orphanage. It had been the most terrifying thing she'd ever experienced. She couldn't go back to that.

"I know it sounds awful, dear," said the housekeeper with a wispy sigh. "But it's better than the streets."

It couldn't be. Bincy dredged up a smile. "Thank you in any case," she said, backing away. "I should be going. You've been very kind."

"Come back here if you don't find anything," the housekeeper called after her. "I'll give you directions to the workhouse."

Bincy ignored her, almost running back down the path and out onto the streets. She wasn't going to the workhouse – she wasn't going to *any* workhouse. She'd have to find a way around this problem.

She didn't have a choice.

THE FIRST NIGHT WAS TERRIFYING. BINCY COULDN'T FIND anywhere to sleep, and she doubted she would have been able to sleep even if she had. She staggered from one street to the next, the pounding fear that clawed and scraped in her belly far more powerful than the exhaustion sucking at her limbs like quicksand. Nightfall had transformed the streets of London into something terrifying. She wasn't sure which was worse: the people that stared at her, or the streets without people, where nothing but emptiness yawned all around her. The refractory ward was the last time she'd been alone, and despite the space around her and the sky above her, she was still more frightened than she'd ever been in her life. It was then that she realized there was something far worse than any pain or fear could ever be: loneliness.

On the second day, she spent two of her three pennies on a chunk of bread that was gone too quickly and sat in her empty stomach like a pebble – hard and insubstantial. When night fell, her legs couldn't carry her any further. She crawled into a doorway, curled up on the step, and slept. She was woken by a policeman's baton and chased, sobbing, down the street. The next place she tried to sleep was the gutter, only to be chased by some rich man's dogs, metal glinting on their luxurious leather collars. She kept going until she reached a slum this time, and nobody asked her any questions there. When she awoke, her left pinky toe was blue and numb. At least it didn't hurt anymore.

On the third day, trembling with weakness and hunger, Bincy spent her final penny on a cup of some gray and nameless soup. She was only halfway through gulping it down when a group of angry boys ran her over, stole the soup and pushed her into the dirt. Crying, she staggered into an alleyway and fell asleep there even though it was before noon. When she woke up in the middle of the night, so cold that she could barely stand up, her toe was black.

By then, the freedom didn't feel exhilarating anymore. It didn't feel like anything anymore. Bincy felt as though her heart had turned to stone. She limped down the street, not knowing where her feet were taking her, not caring either. She was so hungry. She was so cold. Thirst made her want to eat handfuls of the snow lying by the side of the road, but it was so yellowed and filthy that the very thought turned her empty stomach. She retched, but nothing came up.

Hugging herself, she moved on aimlessly, knowing her weak legs couldn't carry her much further. Her chest burned, and every now and then she had to stop and cough up blobs of something greenish from somewhere deep in her lungs. There was so much pain that it had turned into nothingness. The trembling in her muscles forecast an impending collapse, but Bincy welcomed it now. She welcomed darkness.

She welcomed rest.

She was watching her feet moving along the pavement, thinking how strange it was to only have nine good toes, when she noticed it. The cobblestones. They looked so familiar. She stopped, gazing idly down at them, finding it odd how curious she felt. Not even the drunken men that had brawled on the street last night had been able to make her feel anything more than pain and exhaustion, but these cobblestones... there was something about them. She felt like she'd stared at their pattern before, but not directly like this. Through glass. Through a window. Through the window of the orphanage.

Bincy looked up, and there it was, for the first time in five years. The pillared building with its faded inscription above the doorway: PRICE HOME FOR GIRLS. Somehow, her feet had borne her all the way back to the orphanage where she'd grown up.

She knew she was too old to go back as an orphan, but perhaps – just maybe – that glint of warmth she'd seen in Mrs. Price's eyes from time to time would make her feel sorry for her again and give her work. Mrs. Price had to have scullery maids in the kitchen, didn't she? Someone had to wash all of those dishes. Stumbling, dragging her sore foot, Bincy limped up to the doorway. It took the last of her strength to lift the knocker once and allow it to fall back on the door with a flat, final thud.

It took some time before footsteps echoed up that hallway again, the way it had so many years ago when Bincy had clung to the kindly policeman. This time, though, the steps were dragging; she could tell that it wasn't Mrs. Price even before the door opened. But nothing could have prepared her for who it was when she looked up into a pair of fiery eyes that were so familiar, they stopped her heart.

She was older, of course. She had to be about twenty now, considering Bincy was sixteen, and she had grown up as beautiful as her youthful looks had promised. Her flowing hair had been pinned up, her lips painted, her eyes still fiercely bright against her red lips. But the look in those eyes was unmistakable.

It was Mae.

"Well?" she demanded, looking Bincy up and down. "You're too old. Go away."

She began to close the door, and Bincy dived to stop her. "No, please," she gasped. "I know I'm too old to be a resident here. I'm just looking for work. Please."

Mae stopped, giving her a bored look. "What work do you want?"

"I'm a scullery maid. A good one," said Bincy. "I worked for a manor for five years. I can do everything. Please. You must need one," she begged.

"Sorry," said Mae, shrugging. "I filled the last position here when I became a teacher."

A teacher? Mae? Bincy swallowed. "I can teach, too," she said. "I can read. I paid attention to my lessons. Please, I'm starving. Please, Mae. You have to help me."

Mae's eyebrows shot up. "How do you know my name?" she demanded.

That was when Bincy realized Mae didn't recognize her. She stared at her, speechless. Had she really been so fleeting, so insignificant in Mae's life that she wouldn't know her? Or had the past five years changed her so much as to make her unrecognizable?

"You know, don't answer that," said Mae, stepping back. "I already told you. There's no work here." She sneered, making a shooing motion with one elegant hand. "Go back to the slimy streets where you came from, you smelly thing." Wrinkling her delicate nose, she slammed the door. Bincy threw herself against it, sobbing, but she knew that it was no good.

It had never been any good. And Bincy had nowhere left to turn.

CHAPTER 14

Bincy's numbness had turned into blind panic as she stumbled back down the street the way she'd come. It was as if Mae's presence had triggered some primal fear in her, digging up the terror that had been buried under the past few days of hardship. She was going to die on these streets. Death was all around her – in the hunger that made her stomach a hollow pit of pain, the exhaustion that was dragging at her every step, the glints in the eyes of the men who stood in the shadows and watched her scurry past as the sun went down. She would be starved, beaten, frozen. She was going to get killed out here, and she was terrified.

There was only one thing she could think of to do. Only two places in the world had ever been home to her: the orphanage and the Williams manor. Mae had just thrown her out of the orphanage, and the manor was the only choice she had left.

She thought of how that giddy freedom had tasted when she'd walked out four days ago, and the very thought made her sick to her stomach. This wasn't freedom. This was just a new kind of hardship, and she knew exactly what Henry was going to do if she went back, but it was better than this.

It was better than dying like this, alone on these streets.

She'd reached a marketplace that bustled with people, and she stood gazing around at them, feeling utterly bewildered. How was she going to find her way back to the manor? The street names on each corner meant nothing to her; she knew the manor was on Wellington Street, because the sign on the street corner had always been the border of her world, but she had no idea how to get there. She would have to ask someone for directions, but every stranger she saw seemed to be glaring at her like she was something filthy and diseased. Even the homeless man crouched in a shady corner, leering at her with only two teeth in his smile and rheumy eyes, looked terrifying.

That was when she spotted him.

At first, she thought her exhausted mind was playing tricks on her. Surely, it couldn't be – it just couldn't be him. The tall, willowy figure among the crowds belonged to some other young man. It was just coincidence that the hair was exactly the same shade, that the gestures of his hands as he was talking to a stall-holder were so familiar. She stared anyway, because the sight of him brought back a thousand happy memories of their visits in the dark kitchen, of his gentleness with his little sister.

She was still staring, entranced by her memories, when he turned around and she saw his eyes. They were as gray as a rainy day, soft as a down pillow. And when they landed on her, she saw recognition in them.

Bincy couldn't have moved even if she'd wanted to. Rooted to the spot, she stared as he hurried toward her, his eyes widening.

"Bincy!" he called out.

She finally persuaded a sound to come out of her mouth. "Judd?" she whispered.

"I haven't seen you in so long." Judd stood over her, beaming. He had grown taller, and he'd lost that pinched, pale look he'd always had even when Bincy was helping him with food. His face was strong and ruddy, his shoulders broadened.

"It's been years," said Bincy. "I've never stopped worrying about you. I wasn't the one who told on you, Judd. Ada heard us fighting." Tears filled her eyes. "It was my fault, but I never meant for this to happen."

"I know," said Judd, soothingly. He reached out to touch her shoulder gently. "I knew you wouldn't do that, Bincy."

"What happened to you?" Bincy asked, swallowing her tears. "What happened when the police came to fetch you?"

"Luckily Clara and I were both too young to go to jail." Judd struggled to smile. "We were taken to the workhouse instead. She... she wasn't strong enough for it." He looked away, his voice thick with tears. "I know she's safe now, in a better place than this world. She was too good for this city. Too good for this whole planet. But I miss her every single day."

"I'm so sorry."

"It's not your fault." Judd swallowed, looking up at her, a little brighter. "After just a year, a silversmith came to the workhouse looking for an apprentice, and he chose me. I've been working with him ever since. He's very kind."

Bincy felt a rush of relief. Her heart was hurting for Clara, but she knew that Judd was right; there had always been something ethereal about the little girl, a feeling that she wouldn't live long, and Bincy had long suspected that Clara wouldn't make it. But it was so good to see Judd like this: strong and whole, and safe.

"I'm so glad to hear it," she said, grinning up at him. "You deserve to be safe and well."

"And you?" asked Judd. "I've thought about you so often, but I didn't want to go to the manor house in case you got into trouble. Are you still working there?"

Bincy's gut swooped. What was she going to tell Judd? Kind, lovely Judd, who still seemed to think so highly of her? She felt a rush of terrible shame, and suddenly she knew why everyone at the manor house had treated her like she was some kind of disease. She *was* shameful. She felt dirty, tainted by the touch of Henry's hands where she hadn't wanted them.

She couldn't tell Judd about that. She couldn't tell him that he had been right about Henry.

"Oh, yes, I am," she said breezily, stepping back. She looked away, knowing that Judd would read the lie in her eyes if she let him look into them.

"In fact, I'd better get back to work. I just – I'm a little lost. Mrs. Davids sent me out to get some things, and I can't seem to find my way back."

"Let me walk you there," said Judd quickly. "I know the way."

"N-no," Bincy said quickly. "It's all right. I-I don't want to get us both into trouble, like you said."

"That's a good point," said Judd reluctantly. He looked pained but seemed to decide against pushing the issue. "Take this street straight on until you reach the main road. Just follow that for six blocks, then turn to your right. Then you'll be in Wellington Street."

"Thank you," said Bincy. She started to hurry off in the direction he'd pointed.

"Bincy, wait!" Judd called.

Bincy stopped, turning half around. She tried not to look back at him, but her eyes dragged their way up to his, and she saw concern there.

"Are you sure you're all right?" he asked quietly.

"Oh, yes." Bincy forced a smile. "I'm quite sure, thank you. I have to go."

She hurried off as quickly as she could, hoping that he wouldn't follow her. But when he didn't, she felt as though the last ray of sunshine in her life had been quickly, quietly, and brutally snuffed out.

***

When Mrs. Davids opened the door of the servants' entrance, anger filled her so quickly that Bincy thought she would explode.

At that moment, Bincy didn't care. She didn't care if she was caned or beaten or locked in the cupboard for a whole day — she just wanted to get inside to that warm kitchen and sleep on the narrow mattress that had been her bed for years. Despite the terror she knew was waiting for her, all she could feel as she stepped into the manor house was overwhelming relief.

So, when Mrs. Davids inflated her chest, ready to shriek out her rage, Bincy didn't flinch. She just stood there looking up at her, resigned to her fate.

When Mrs. Davids finally spoke, though, the screech of rage that Bincy was waiting for never came. Instead, her voice was flat, trembling slightly with the weight of her fury. "You had better come in."

Bincy stared at her as Mrs. Davids stepped back, opening the door. "What?"

"I said come in," growled Mrs. Davids between clenched teeth.

Bincy didn't know what to think, but she was too tired and hungry to argue. She walked slowly into the kitchen, emotions swamping her as she looked around the small, gray space. She'd only been away for less than a week, but it felt like centuries; despite the fear of what could happen lurking in every corner, despite the foul smell of unwashed dishes, it was the closest thing to home that she knew.

"Let me make one thing clear to you, girl." Mrs. Davids grabbed her arm, spinning her around. Suddenly they were nose to nose, and Mrs. Davids's voice was still low and sinuous as a snake on the dirt. "If it was up to me, you'd be thrown into the deepest, darkest dungeon in this entire forsaken city. You'd be hanged for your filthiness."

As if remembering that Bincy was infectious somehow, she jerked her hand away and glared down at her in disgust. "You're just lucky that your young man friend from the manor house left me with the strictest orders that you should be let in if you return. I was hoping you wouldn't. I hoped the dogs would eat you out there on that street." She was almost pop-eyed with anger now. "He's away visiting some friends for the next few days, but he'll be back. Maybe then, you'll get what you deserve."

Bincy's stomach knotted at Mrs. Davids's words. She swallowed hard, and the housekeeper stepped back. "Get out of my sight," she said. "I'll expect the fires to be lit already when we come down to the scullery at five o' clock tomorrow morning."

"Yes, ma'am," Bincy whispered.

"Don't speak." Mrs. Davids held up a hand. "Just do it."

Not knowing where else to go, Bincy slunk off to the servants' quarters and fell down on her pallet. She dropped the cloth bag of her belongings beside her. The book shifted open slightly, and a corner of the lavender slipped out, dusting the page lightly. She gazed at it, too numb to think about what it meant. What coming back here meant, and what was going to happen to her.

The door to her room crashed open. Bincy startled, sitting up. Silhouetted in the doorway, Ada was trembling with rage, her frizzy hair standing out around her head like snakes. Bincy couldn't see her face, but she didn't need to. She knew that pure anger would be shining in her eyes.

"I can't believe it," Ada cried out. She spat on the ground and called Bincy by a name that made her heart break at the injustice of it. Then, striding nearer, Ada seized Bincy by the hair.

"Ow!" Bincy yelped, grabbing at Ada's wrist as she was dragged out of the pallet.

Ada slapped her hand away. "Mrs. Davids might be too scared of that young master to give you what you deserve," she growled, "but I'm not."

"Let me go!" Bincy yelped.

Ada's slap split her lip again on the same place as before. Bincy closed her eyes, whimpering in pain and fear, as Ada seized a belt from where it was lying on her own bed.

"You need to learn a lesson," she hissed in Bincy's face, saliva spraying on her cheek. "And there's only one way to teach it to you."

Bincy closed her eyes. And with every blow, she told herself it could have been worse.

She could have been Clara.

※

THE BRUISES ON BINCY'S NECK AND SHOULDERS MADE EVEN the small movements of polishing the silver difficult. She was too tired to flinch as she worked the cloth and polish over the delicate soup spoon in her hand, rubbing away the tarnish to make the metal gleam. Holding it up to the light, Bincy saw her reflection in the shiny metal. There was a black bruise on her cheek, and even though it had been days since her return to the Williams manor, there was still an ugly scab on her bottom lip.

The only bright side she could find was that she was still alive.

She could feel the anger and disapproval radiating from the cook, even though the old woman's back was turned as she filleted a fish by the kitchen table. Bincy sighed inwardly, laying the spoon back in its drawer. It was no use to plead her case. Everyone had already made up their minds about her, and her days were going to be one moment of dread after the other as she waited for Henry to get back – and once he was back... She took a deep breath. Maybe it wouldn't be so bad. Maybe it would be better than she'd thought. Maybe her fears were unfounded.

Or maybe she should have frozen to death on the street.

When Henry's voice spoke in the doorway, Bincy thought she was imagining it. She shook her head sharply, trying to clear her tired mind, trying to tell her racing heart that she was hearing things. Then he spoke again.

"I said get out."

Bincy spun around. Henry was standing in the door, his eyes furious, but he wasn't looking at her. He was glaring at the cook and Ada. They both shot Bincy a venomous look before heading out into the hall that led to the servants' quarters. As soon as they were both gone, Henry hurried over to her. She spun around, wanting to hold out her hands to stop him, her body as tight as the strings on the violin she'd seen a few days ago. But to her surprise, when Henry's hands landed on her shoulders, they were gentle.

She cringed, waiting for him to demand where she'd gone. Instead, the old Henry was in his eyes again – a softness that she hadn't been expecting.

"What happened to you?" he asked.

Bincy swallowed. There was no point in lying, nor could she think of anything to say. "Ada," she whispered.

Henry's expression darkened again, and that glimpse of the sweet boy she'd fallen in love with was gone. "The kitchen maid?"

"Yes."

Henry gritted his teeth. "If only I had the power to do it, I would have her burned at the stake," he snarled. His fingers caressed her bruised cheek. "Nobody is allowed to lift a finger against my little hidden treasure."

Bincy felt herself relax slightly. Had he gotten over whatever had made him so strange the past few weeks?

"I'm sorry I left," she whispered, feeling tears gathering in her eyes. "I'm so sorry. I... I..."

"It's all right, treasure," said Henry. He moved closer, and his eyes were burning again. "You're back now." He whispered the words against her skin. "You're mine again now." His hands crept up her back, reaching her shoulder blades. She tried to move back, and he followed, pinning her against the kitchen table. "And you will be mine, all mine," he murmured.

"You're hurting me," Bincy whimpered as Henry gripped her arms, squeezing her bruises. But if Henry heard, he didn't care. His lips found hers, working across her mouth, violent and passionate, sending stabs of burning pain across her split lower lip.

She felt suffocated, crushed against the table as Henry's hands roamed over her, unfettered by any kind of consideration. They went to the buttons on her dress again and her stomach swooped. It was happening. He was taking her. But, to her surprise, there they stopped. He pulled back, looking at her with a savage grin, panting.

"Not today," he said breathlessly. "No. We'll let your bruised little body heal up first." He put a finger under her chin and forced her head up so he could kiss her lips again. "But be ready for the day that I send for you." He stepped back, grinning. "I'll see you soon, treasure."

He almost skipped out of the kitchen, and Bincy fled back to her quarters, tears cascading down her cheeks.

CHAPTER 15

Bincy didn't go back to the kitchen all afternoon. Nor did anybody come back to send for her. Henry had made her untouchable – to everyone except him, in any case.

It was dark now, and Ada was snoring gently in the bed beside Bincy's, but she still stared at the ceiling.

"You should be grateful," she whispered to herself. "Isn't this everything you wanted? Henry in love with you, and nobody able to hurt you because of this. This must be what he meant when he said he'd give me a better life."

Tears prickled behind her eyes. Whatever Henry was feeling when he gripped her, when he kissed her, it didn't feel like love. Bincy rolled over, squeezing her eyes tightly shut. What was love, really?

She'd thought Mama had loved her, but then she'd been abandoned in the marketplace. Mrs. Price might have cared for her and the other orphans, but she'd locked Bincy in the refractory ward and then dragged her out to the manor house where she was lying now, sobbing quietly. Mae had tolerated her, but Bincy knew she'd never loved her. And she'd thought Henry was in love with her, yet he didn't care about hurting her. It made her wonder what love really was.

It made her wonder if love existed at all.

She was half falling asleep as the memory swam back up to the surface. It was of Judd – years ago, with little Clara in his arms, her head tucked beneath his chin. The way he'd held that little girl, as if she were made of the most precious and fragile China. It was so different from the way Henry's hands felt on Bincy's body. The way he'd spoken to her, as if he wanted his words to warm every corner of his tiny, fragile sister's heart. If there was love in the world, then Bincy had glimpsed it only once. And it had been between Judd and Clara. Judd would have done anything to protect his little sister – he'd turn the whole world inside out for her.

She should have told him everything, she thought, when she'd come across him on the street a few days ago. He would have helped her the same way she'd helped him and Clara. But what could she say? Could she tell him how Henry treated her? Could she tell him she'd allowed it? She turned her head into the pillow, choking back a sob. Judd would hate her for it. She couldn't bear the shame of telling him such a thing.

The bell rang, and Bincy rose, her eyes sleepless and sandy. As it was now, the only mercy in her life was that her bruises were still painful and obvious, not yet healed. But she knew they would heal. And after that, she couldn't bear to think of what would happen next.

***

Her bruises took a week to heal. Every morning that Bincy got dressed and saw them fading from blue to green to yellow to healthy, pink flesh, her dread grew. She knew that it was only a matter of time before Henry's mood turned in her direction, and she would be summoned up to his room.

When the morning dawned with the information that Henry's parents were going out for dinner, Bincy knew the day had come. She dragged herself through her daily tasks, living in the bubble of cold isolation that Henry had constructed for her. The day felt a thousand years long. It seemed to take centuries to wash the dishes, peel the carrots, take out the garbage.

It was almost dark when Bincy was walking back from where she'd disposed of the garbage and heard the clatter of hooves coming up the street. Barely interested through her fog of despair, she looked up to see a fine four-in-hand galloping up to the Williams manor, their flanks foaming white with sweat, sparks flying from their iron-rimmed hooves. A whip cracked, and a drunken young voice urged them on until they reached the gate of the manor.

The driver hauled back on the reins, and the horses skidded to a halt, the wheels of the carriage squealing behind them. It tipped for a moment, teetering dangerously on two wheels for a second, before crashing back down onto all fours. The horses were gasping and champing as they jostled each other, held back by the reins, but desperate to flee. Bincy knew exactly how they felt.

The door of the carriage crashed open, and Henry tumbled out with a group of his friends. His hair was in disarray, his tie missing, his shirt unbuttoned so that his curling golden chest hairs were easily visible in the setting sunlight. He was swaying as he raised a hand to greet the driver. Bincy couldn't make out the words, but she could hear that he was slurring his words.

She watched as the driver wrenched the horses around and lashed them back up to a gallop again. Following his friends, Henry turned to stumble his way back toward the manor house, and as he did so, he spotted her. He stopped, gazing at her for a moment, his face slack and expressionless, but there was a gleam in his eyes, and Bincy knew. Then he staggered back up toward the house.

Bincy gazed up the long, empty street again. Perhaps she should just start walking. Walk and never turn back. But a chill breeze rustled down between the houses, sending eddies of snow swirling, rising up to touch her face with a kiss that was as cold as death. She shuddered and turned back to walk into the kitchen.

It wasn't long before Ada came into the scullery, her face as twisted as if she'd just taken a mouthful of acid. Bincy turned away, but Ada grabbed her shoulder and spun her around to face her. Mute, Bincy stared into her eyes. Nothing could bring her to feel more terror than she already had in her heart.

Ada spat the words. "He wants you," she said, then followed it up with a crudity that couldn't hurt Bincy now, because she knew the words were true. She was about to live up to it, to walk up to that room and become something completely different. She had no idea what she'd wanted to be in life. Loved, perhaps. But whatever it was, she hadn't wanted this.

What choice did she have? She put down the mop and bucket she'd been using and walked toward the door. She'd only been in the rest of the manor house a few times, when they were short-staffed after losing the parlor maid to consumption, but she knew the way to Henry's room. Her feet left the cold stone of the kitchen floor behind and found a soft, deep carpet. It was almost luxurious. Maybe her life would become luxurious now, too. It wouldn't be so bad. In fact, she knew she couldn't hope for anything better.

She reached the landing, gazed up at the stairs, and stopped. There was no one in the big room now except her, staring up at those carpeted stairs, illuminated by a sparkling chandelier. Gazing up at those sparkles, Bincy was reminded of the light in Judd's eyes when he looked at Clara. The gentleness in the way he held his sister. The respect in the way he spoke to Bincy. And something shattered inside her, opening a flood of something that burned like anger.

"No," she said, aloud. Her voice echoed around the empty room, giving her courage. "No. There is something better in the world than this." She stepped back. Her heart was hammering, but for the first time, the pounding was hope instead of fear. "There is real love in the world, and I've seen it. And I want it. And I can do better than this." She gulped. "I don't deserve this. I did nothing wrong. And I won't let myself be taken like this."

There was nobody in the room to hear her speech, but she heard it, and that was all that mattered. Her toes and fingers were tingling, and she felt as though her spirit was soaring, ripping itself free from the shackles that had held it for so long. She didn't think. She just spun around and began to run, toward the big main doors, toward the outside world with all its chaos and despair and that dizzy freedom that could mean death, or it could mean life, but at least it never meant bondage. Bincy Hall was done with bondage, once and for all.

Her outstretched hands met the main doors and they clanged

open, and the world was thrown wide before her, the terrifying and glorious world where she could do and become anything she decided to be. This time when the cold wind blew in her face, she welcomed it, relished it as she ran forward, sucked it in despite the way it burned her fragile lungs. And as she ran into the street, she was laughing, despite it all, because she knew that she could die out here tonight. But at least she would be dying on her own terms.

"HEY!" The cry came from a top window. Bincy looked up and saw Henry's reddened face glaring out of it. "Where are you going?" he roared.

Bincy laughed, throwing her arms wide as she spun in the snow. She felt deliciously insane. "Away from you!" she hollered. "I don't need you!"

Henry stared at her, his mouth hanging open. Bincy turned to walk away, her head held high for the first time in her entire life. Then he shrieked again. "THIEF!" he thundered. "Stop thief! Stop that girl!"

There was yelling from inside the house and the thunder of feet rushing down the stairs. Bincy wasn't afraid, but she knew she should run. She spun and bolted up the street as fast as she could, hearing the screams around her as Henry and his friends tumbled out in a frenzy of rage.

"Go after her!" she heard Henry shout. "I'm fetching my horse! Groom, get my horse!"

Loud footsteps came up behind her, and Bincy redoubled her pace, heading for the end of the street as fast as her legs would carry her. When she reached it, she turned hard left and bolted toward the busy marketplace. Perhaps she'd lose them in the crowd. Perhaps she wouldn't, but either way, she would not surrender.

She heard their shouts growing louder behind her and knew how much faster they were than she was. Women shrieked in panic on the street as she whizzed past them, children pointing, horses shying wildly as she pushed between the traffic in the falling dusk. Voices were yelling angrily, but behind her they only intensified, "Thief! Stop thief!"

Bincy wasn't going to stop. She was going to run herself to death if she had to, but she was going to get away from them. She pushed through a group of horsemen, dived underneath a stationary carriage and bolted down an alleyway, but they were hot on her heels. Then she heard galloping hoofbeats behind her and Henry's voice.

"You're not going to get away from me!" he shouted. "You're never going to escape!"

She wanted to shout something back, something ugly and defiant, but she was too focused on running. They were on the main road now, and there was more traffic, but she ran up against it, her eyes fixed on the horizon. Henry was yelling, the sound of a whip striking horseflesh right behind her. He was gaining on her. He was gaining on her, and for the first time since walking out of the manor house, Bincy felt fear. Her legs were going numb with exhaustion, her heart thrashing in her chest. Maybe it would burst before he caught her.

She swung a little to the right, leaving the road, crashing onto the sidewalk. A group of women yelped in panic as she pushed between them, trying to disappear among them. Henry's voice behind her turned angrily puzzled. Perhaps it was going to work, if only she could put on one more burst of speed and reach the end of the street—

The hands came out of nowhere. One seized her by the arm, yanking her to the right so hard that something wrenched in her shoulder. She would have screamed if the other hand hadn't slapped down on her face, clapping her mouth closed. Panicking, Bincy thrashed, but her limbs were weak with exhaustion. She could do nothing to stop herself from being dragged into an alleyway that was filled with nothing but darkness. She felt her body being pulled back, pressed against something that was solid and panting, a man. Her heart swooped. She'd just run out of the frying pan to land in the fire.

There was breath on her neck, and it made every hair in her body stand up. No! She was going to fight this! She struck out blindly with a hand, and that was when he spoke.

"Bincy! Hush. It's only me. Hush now so that they'll go past without knowing that you're here."

Bincy froze.

She knew that voice.

CHAPTER 16

Only after the angry voices and galloping hoofbeats had disappeared into the distance did he gently release his grip on Bincy's arm and face. She whirled around to stare up at him. It was so dark that she could only see the whites of his eyes and the curve of his smile.

"I'm sorry I scared you," he said. "I just had to get you away from them without them seeing where you'd gone."

"Judd?" Bincy whispered. "Could it really be you?"

Judd stepped forward. The slanting golden light from the lamp-post just outside the alleyway fell across his face, and his eyes were shining just like that chandelier, just like the way they always used to shine when he looked down at Clara. He didn't touch her. Instead, he said simply, "Yes. It's me."

"Oh, Judd." Bincy couldn't help it. She lurched forward, her arms wrapped around herself, and simply pressed herself into his arms. He hesitated for a moment, then wrapped his arms around her, leaning his head on top of hers, tucking her under his chin like she was a little girl.

"It's all right now," he said softly, rubbing her back. "You're safe now. Nothing is going to hurt you ever again. I promise."

With all her heart, Bincy believed him. She allowed herself to sob for a few minutes, her face buried against her chest. The freedom she'd felt running from the manor house was still pounding in her, but it was slower now, more rhythmic, like something that was here to stay.

She pulled back and stared up at Judd. "How did you find me?"

"How could I not?" Judd smiled. "I was worried about you."

"Why?"

"I've seen you tired before, Bincy. But the way you looked when we bumped into one another in the marketplace that day, I knew something was wrong. You didn't look well at all." Concern filled his eyes. "I knew you were in trouble somehow."

Trouble. Bincy felt her cheeks reddening. She hoped that Judd didn't know how right he was.

"I started to hang around the manor again," he went on.

"Making sure that no one would see me, but just trying to keep an eye on you. I was on my way back home when I heard the yelling and saw you running."

"I'm so glad you did," said Bincy, forcing a smile. Her thoughts were spinning. What was she going to tell Judd when he asked her what was going on?

He didn't ask her, though. He just reached for her hand and took it, but his fingers didn't interlace with hers; the steady pressure on her palm was almost fatherly. "Do you want to go back to the manor?" he asked gently.

Bincy shook her head. "No."

"All right. Then you can come with me, if you want. I stay with the silversmith that I'm working for. They've got a room ready for you."

"A room?" Bincy blinked. "Why?"

"I thought you might want to leave," said Judd. "And they're good people. Only if you want to come with me, though."

Even if Bincy had another choice, she suddenly wanted nothing more than to hold on to Judd's hand and allow him to lead her somewhere safe. To a room of her own. "Yes, please," she said quietly.

"Come on, then." Judd squeezed her hand lightly and headed back out onto the street. "It's not a long walk."

Bincy was grateful to hear those words. She followed Judd

quietly through the streets, enjoying the fact that not a single man even looked at her now that she was closely by Judd's side. He took her through the marketplace and into an area of the city she'd never seen before. The houses here were small – more like cottages, to be honest – but they were clean and tidy, the little fences around their small plots all standing upright, the narrow street newly swept. Judd went up to a small, double-story house with firelight in the windows and a cheerful twist of woodsmoke in the chimney.

"Mr. Fernsby," he called out. "It's me."

The door opened immediately, revealing a rotund gentleman in a brass-buttoned waistcoat who wore a monocle and had enormous white whiskers. His eyes were twinkling as he looked down at Bincy.

"Is this the girl you've told us about, Judd?" he asked.

"The very same," said Judd. He let go of Bincy's hand. "I found her just in time."

At that point, an older lady with her white hair caught up in a bun appeared beside the man. "Oh, you poor dear!" she cried.

To Bincy's astonishment, she lunged forward, grabbed Bincy's hand, and more or less dragged her into the cottage.

"Come, come. You look like you need a good, square meal, don't you? Oh, and a lovely bath. And look at your dress! It'll need a wash and a mend. Never fear, my darling, you're about the same size as our Mary, who's all grown and has children besides, but there must still be one or two of her things in the house, don't you think?"

All of these words came out at once, as shiny and floating as soap bubbles, and Bincy found herself thrust into a kitchen chair and clutching a mug of hot tea before she really knew what was going on. Judd followed her inside, and Mr. Fernsby closed the door behind them.

"Tut, tut!" His wife regarded Bincy sorrowfully for a moment, then shook her head as she hurried to the stove. "Such a disheveled little thing! I can't wait to get a comb through that hair, my dear. But first things first, don't you think? Some good, hearty stew would be just the thing. You need a nice full stomach, and then everything will be all right, don't you think?"

"I think," said Judd, laughing at Bincy's expression, "that perhaps some introductions are in order, Mrs. Fernsby."

"Oh, of course! What a fool I am." Mrs. Fernsby stopped and twinkled down at Bincy for a moment. "I'm Patricia Fernsby, dear. And this is my husband, Flavius Fernsby. And I take it you know our darling Judd." She pinched Judd's cheek as if he was a little boy. "What would we do without him?"

Judd laughed, his eyes shining with fondness. "What would I do without you?" he asked. "Mr. and Mrs. Fernsby came to the workhouse for a 'prentice, and they saved my life when they took me back to learn Mr. Fernsby's trade. I would have gone crazy in that place before long, with dear Clara gone."

Mr. Fernsby shook his head. "A terrible place, that workhouse," he said. "Just terrible."

"But let's not talk about that," said Mrs. Fernsby. "It's all behind us now, and this darling girl doesn't want to hear about all those things, don't you think?" The three words bloomed like a flower at the end of her sentence, and Bincy found them rather endearing. "And you *must* be Bincy, dear. Judd has never stopped talking about you."

Bincy blushed, looking up sideways at Judd. He wouldn't meet her eyes, but she thought there was some extra color in his cheeks, too.

"Are you sure she can stay for just a while, Mrs. Fernsby?" he asked. "I'm sorry to impose, but there's nowhere else…"

"My dear, we have enough to go around," said Mrs. Fernsby firmly. "We'll find her a good position soon, I know it, and until then, I daresay she'll be a helpful little thing to have around the house. Don't you worry about a thing."

"I'll forever be grateful, Mrs. Fernsby," said Judd.

"Years and years ago, a kindly housekeeper gave me a chance," said Mrs. Fernsby, smiling fondly. "She came to fetch me from a workhouse just like we did with you, and if it wasn't for her, I would never have survived. I always vowed I'd return the favor someday, and I'm only too happy to do that."

Bincy didn't know what to say, so she didn't say anything for the rest of the evening, which was a wild bewilderment of warmth and food and joy and conversation like she'd never heard or seen before. She was given a bowl of stew so big that she thought she might explode if she finished it, but she promptly polished it off. Then Mrs. Fernsby bundled her off to a bathroom where she was stuffed into a tin bath and scrubbed and scrubbed until she felt human again while Mrs. Fernsby slowly combed out her hair, piece by piece, so that it fell around her shoulders in a soft, golden cloud. Wrapped in a towel, she waited until Mrs. Fernsby brought her a linen gown, which lay against her curves with the familiarity of a tender hug.

Finally, she was led up the stairs to a landing. Mrs. Fernsby squeezed her hand. "Here's your room, dear," she said, pushing open a door to reveal a small room with a little round window, a candle on the bedside table, and a bed – a real one, with a soft mattress and feather covers, not a bunk or a pallet. Bincy stared at it. "Just say if you need anything." With that, Mrs. Fernsby gave her a friendly pat on the shoulder and bustled off.

Bincy was still standing in the doorway, just staring, when she heard soft footsteps behind her. She didn't have to turn around to know that it was Judd.

"You can go inside, you know," he said, softly. "It's for you."

Bincy wanted to step forward and slide under those warm covers, but something was stopping her. The linen was white – perfectly starched. She knew that her skin was clean, but she couldn't shake the feeling that if she so much as touched that white linen, she would stain it with the truth of what Henry had almost done.

That was when she spoke at last for the first time since coming into this perfect, beautiful little cottage with its wonderful people. She turned to face him, gazing at his kind eyes. "I'm sorry, Judd," she whispered. "I can't stay."

His face fell, but he tried to hide it. "Why not?" he asked. "What's wrong?"

"I don't deserve it." Bincy swallowed hard against the lump in her throat. "I-I didn't tell you why I ran from the manor, Judd. It wasn't because they were starving me or hurting me." She felt the tears spill over. "You were right," she admitted at last. "Henry didn't have good intentions. He..." She couldn't finish the sentence.

"Shhh." Judd touched her shoulder. "I know. They know, too. It's not your fault, Bincy. We still want to help you." He cleared his throat. "*I* still want to help you."

Bincy stared up at him. "Promise?"

Judd's smile, in that moment, was her world.

"I promise," he said again.

So many promises had been broken. But this one tasted solid and real, and Bincy held it close in her heart as she closed the door behind her, slid between the covers, and sank into the deepest sleep she'd ever known.

⁂

Bincy's stomach growled in anticipation as she bent down in front of the oven. She pulled on the oven gloves as if she was arming herself for battle. "I'm not sure about them, Mrs. Fernsby," she said worriedly. "I've never baked anything before."

"You've been cooking for three weeks, love," said Mrs. Fernsby behind her, laying a maternal hand on her shoulder. "You've done so well. I'm sure they'll be nice – and if they aren't, why, then we'll just try again, that's all."

Encouraged, Bincy opened the oven and drew out the tray of scones. She put them down on the kitchen table and gave them a critical look. "They don't look that bad."

"Not at all. Let's see how they taste." Mrs. Fernsby levered one out with a knife. Steam burst from the fluffy inside as she cut it open and sliced off a piece. She held it up to the light, and Bincy felt a rush of pride as she saw that it was golden and light. "Beautiful!" she said. "It's going to be delicious." With that, she confidently popped it into her mouth.

Bincy saw immediately that something was wrong. Mrs. Fernsby's eyes began to water. Her face grew redder and redder, but she continued to chew valiantly on the scone, her eyes streaming. "What is it?" asked Bincy. "What's wrong?"

With a courageous effort, Mrs. Fernsby choked it down. "It's – it's very nice, dear," she croaked.

Bincy grabbed a piece of the scone. "It doesn't look like it," she said, and gulped it down. Immediately, a strong flavor of salt grabbed her by the back of the tongue, making her gag. "Ugh!" she yelped, struggling to swallow it. "That's awful!"

"No, no!" Mrs. Fernsby coughed. "They're all right, love. They just need a little less salt."

Bincy looked up at the kindly old lady's red face and couldn't help it. She burst out laughing, and Mrs. Fernsby joined her. Their mirth bounced and tumbled around the little kitchen in the afternoon light.

"All right," said Mrs. Fernsby, wiping away tears of laughter. "They are terrible. But never you mind, dear. We'll just make another batch, that's all."

They were still laughing when the door opened and Mr. Fernsby came in, closely followed by Judd. "Hello, my pretty!" he said, swooping in to kiss Mrs. Fernsby's cheek. "Did you have a nice day?"

"Lovely," said Mrs. Fernsby.

Bincy looked shyly over at Judd. He gave her a smile that

made her heart flip over, and she lowered her eyes, feeling a flutter of joy in her stomach.

"I have some good news to share with you" said Mr. Fernsby. "Especially with you, Bincy."

Bincy looked up. "Is it about a job, sir?" she asked.

"It is indeed. And I think it would be utterly perfect for you," said Mr. Fernsby. "My darling sister, Agatha, is married to a lovely man who is a businessman. He has to travel to India for a year for his business, you see, and they don't have any children. Agatha is going to need a personal maid and companion to stay with her. You'll need to help with some cooking and cleaning, of course, but you'll also be able to improve your education and just spend time with the old girl – she mustn't be lonely. There is good pay, too. She was asking around, and I said you would be perfect for the job, and she said that if I recommended you, you're already hired – if you want the job, of course."

Bincy grinned up at Judd, who lit up at the sight of her happiness. "Of course, I do!" she said. "It'll be just perfect! I'd be so happy to work for someone as nice as you."

"I can assure you that Agatha is considerably nicer," said Mr. Fernsby, laughing. "There's just one catch, though, my dear. You see, Agatha lives out in the country. You would have to go and stay with her." His expression was sympathetic as his eye wandered from Bincy to Judd. "You wouldn't be able to see each other for a year, except when Agatha comes to London to see me."

Bincy felt a quick jolt of fear. She looked up at Judd, thinking of the pure and precious thing that was slowly growing between them, so unlike what she'd had with Henry. Henry had been a raging wildfire; what she had with Judd was just a spark now, but she felt it could grow into the steady warmth of a blaze in the hearth. Would this distance be enough to snuff it out?

Judd reached for her hand. For the first time, their fingers intertwined. "I will always be here waiting for you," he said softly.

Bincy smiled. It was the first time in her life that courage came naturally. "I know you will be," she said.

"Then that's all settled," said Mr. Fernsby. "How magnificent! And look at these delightful scones!"

"No!" cried Mrs. Fernsby and Bincy together, but it was too late. Mr. Fernsby had already stuffed an entire scone in his mouth. As the kitchen filled with laughter, Mr. Fernsby coughing and spluttering in the midst of it, Bincy felt something new blossoming in her soul. Something so novel and lovely that it took her a few minutes to remember its name.

Hope.

CHAPTER 17

One Year Later

THIS WAS THE LAST STOP. AS BINCY CLIMBED DOWN OFF the coach, she was relieved to recognize her surroundings at last. As beautiful as the rolling hills and patchwork fields of the countryside were, London had always been her home, and as she gazed around the marketplace, she felt embraced by the walls of the shops on all sides.

She turned around, scanning the faces of the crowd all around her. Her surroundings were familiar, but none of the faces were. She felt a pang of fear and looked down at the letter that was clutched in her hand. It was signed, *With all my love, your own Judd.* A time was written higher up in the letter: *3:00 p. m.* She looked up at the church clock that towered above the marketplace just as it struck the third hour.

"Where are you, Judd?" Bincy murmured, shading her eyes to look around. For a second, the ground seemed to teeter under her feet. She felt seven years old again and abandoned.

"Don't be silly," Bincy told herself, shaking her head. "He's been waiting all year for you to get back. He's not going to leave... you..."

That was when she saw a face she recognized. But it didn't belong to Judd. In fact, Bincy hadn't seen it for so long that she was surprised it looked familiar at all. It was deeply lined, the hair above gray, but when the woman turned around, she recognized the eyes. They had been blue once, but now appeared watered down. Squeezed by hardship.

Bincy stepped forward, hardly believing her eyes. "Mama?"

The woman stopped. Her eyes focused on Bincy's, and Bincy saw her jaw drop. She stepped back, and for a moment, Bincy thought she would hurry away, would melt into the crowd the way she'd done more than ten years ago when she'd abandoned Bincy to her fate. A fate that had almost been worse than death. For a moment, Bincy almost hoped she would run away. Instead, she started to walk over. There was a hitch in her gait, a half-limp, but she moved as quickly as she could until she was mere inches from Bincy.

"Bincy?" she murmured. "Can it be? After all these years?"

Bincy nodded. "Yes, Mama," she said softly. "It is."

Mama took a cautious step closer, skittish as a wild thing. She reached up, her fingertips just barely brushing Bincy's cheek. "You've grown."

"I have, Mama. I'm eighteen now."

"Eighteen." Mama shook her head. Emotions flitted over her face like cloud shadows on a windy day. "Are you safe?"

"Yes, Mama." Bincy smiled at her. "I'm perfectly safe."

Mama's eyes misted, and Bincy saw her shoulders relax. The movement was almost rusty, as if it had been years since she'd last allowed them to do that. "That's... that's good," she said. "That is so, so good."

For a few more moments, they just gazed at each other, Mama drinking Bincy in. Then she stepped back, the skittishness coming back into her movements. "I have to go," she said. "I-I'm sorry." She paused. "Bincy, I'm sorry I left you. I'm sorry I can't stay."

"It's all right, Mama," said Bincy. The words came naturally, flowing straight from her heart. "I forgive you." She smiled, squaring her shoulders. "And I don't need you." There was no anger in her tone. "I needed you for many, many years and you weren't there, but I forgive you for all of it, and I'm all right now. I don't need you anymore."

Mama smiled. Bincy wondered if this was the first and only

time she'd ever seen her mother smile. "That's good," she whispered.

Then she was gone, but it was all right because Judd was running across the marketplace toward her, looking at her as if she were his entire world. Bincy gave a cry of joy, dropping her case as she ran toward him and leapt into his arms. He didn't spin her. He just caught her and held her close, breathing her in for a few seconds before he set her onto her feet.

"I've missed you so much," Bincy cried.

"I know, my love." Judd kissed her forehead. "I've missed you, too. But it's all over now. No more longing." His eyes sparkled. "Mr. Fernsby says that Agatha gave you such good references, there are three ladies asking after you to employ you as a housekeeper."

Bincy laughed. "And Mrs. Fernsby tells me that you're a silversmith yourself now."

"I am." Judd grinned. "And do you know what that means?"

"Hmm." Bincy pretended to think for a moment. "It means you can make silver things?"

"Bincy!" Judd laughed, then paused to kiss her cheek. "It means we can get married now, love. And we can rent a beautiful little house and have beautiful little children. And you will be my beautiful, perfect little wife."

Bincy leaned against him, breathing his smell. It was the smell of home.

"I can't wait," she said.

Then she took his hand, and they walked away into the busy streets.

THE END

CONTINUE READING...

Thank you for reading **The Forsaken Maid's Secret! Are you wondering what to read next?** Why not read **Thief Girl? Here's a sneak peek for you:**

Ivy clutched her grandmother's skirt, the cheap material rough and dirty in her little hands. She tried her best to hide behind Granny's legs, but a withered hand closed over her shoulder, and she found herself being pushed forward.

"Come on, child," hissed Granny. "Stop your foolishness."

Ivy whimpered, pulling up a piece of Granny's skirt to cover her face. She didn't know the woman who was standing on the doorstep, and she didn't want to, either. She just wanted to go back to her corner of the kitchen and curl up on her blanket and sleep. But she couldn't tell that to her grandmother.

"Do you see what I have to put up with?" said Granny, exasperated. She straightened, loosening her grip on Ivy's shoulder. "I don't know what's the matter with this child. She hardly speaks a word or looks at anyone. She's no use to me whatsoever."

"Oh, Mama, is that really the point?" asked the woman on the step.

Now safely hidden behind Granny's legs, Ivy dared to peer around her knees, giving the woman a quick glance. She was scrawny and weathered; her face so brown and wrinkled that it looked like a piece of old leather that had been left out in the sun for too long. Her lips were chapped, and her gnarled hands were roughly wrapped in bits of rags. She had them planted on her hips, and her filthy hair seemed to be a dull shade of red beneath the coating of grime that covered her from head to toe. Ivy didn't dare to look at her eyes.

"The point, Bertha, is that I'm much too old to be running after you girls," Granny griped. "You both were supposed to have provided for me in my old age. Worked my fingers to the bone, I did, trying to get you two some kind of a future or even an education." She snorted. "And look where that got me. One daughter comes home pregnant, gives birth to the child, and disappears. And the other..."

"The other what?" asked Bertha sharply, raising her chin. Ivy huddled back behind Granny's legs.

"We all know what it is that you do, Bertha."

"What's it to you?" Bertha flipped her red hair defiantly. "At least, I'm in a better trade than my sister – assuming she got pregnant the way that I think she did."

"Stealing is hardly any better," snapped Granny.

Bertha looked away, going quiet. Ivy glanced up at her; she was gazing down the street, her eyes filled with tears. She stared into the distance for a few long, silent moments before turning back to Granny. Ivy shrank back. "I didn't come here today to argue with you," she said coldly.

"No, I suppose you didn't." Granny sighed. "I've done my bit of cleaning up your sister's mess. Now it's your turn."

Visit Here to Continue Reading:

http://www.ticahousepublishing.com/victorian-romance.html

THANKS FOR READING

If you **love Victorian Romance**, **Click Here:**

https://victorian.subscribemenow.com/

to hear about all **New Faye Godwin Romance Releases!** I will let you know as soon as they become available!

Thank you, Friends! If you enjoyed ***The Forsaken Maid's Secret*** would you kindly take a couple minutes to leave a positive review on Amazon? It only takes a moment, and positive reviews truly make a difference. Thank you so much! I appreciate it!

Much love,

Faye Godwin

MORE FAYE GODWIN VICTORIAN ROMANCES!

We love rich, dramatic Victorian Romances and have a library of Faye Godwin titles just for you! (Remember that ALL of Faye's Victorian titles can be downloaded FREE with Kindle Unlimited!)

VISIT HERE to discover Faye's Complete Collection of Victorian Romance:

http://ticahousepublishing.com/victorian-romance.html

ABOUT THE AUTHOR

Faye Godwin has been fascinated with Victorian Romance since she was a teen. After reading every Victorian Romance in her public library, she decided to start writing them herself —which she's been doing ever since. Faye lives with her husband and young son in England. She loves to travel throughout her country, dreaming up new plots for her romances. She's delighted to join the Tica House Publishing family and looks forward to getting to know her readers.

contact@ticahousepublishing.com

Printed in Great Britain
by Amazon